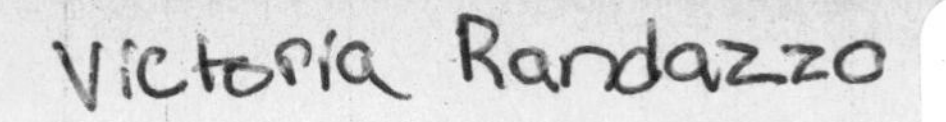

i am the wallpaper

ALSO BY MARK PETER HUGHES

Lemonade Mouth

markpeterhughes

Delacorte Press

Published by Delacorte Press
an imprint of Random House Children's Books
a division of Random House, Inc.
New York

www.randomhouse.com/teens

Educators and librarians, for a variety of teaching tools, visit us at
www.randomhouse.com/teachers

The Library of Congress has cataloged the hardcover edition of this work as follows:

Hughes, Mark Peter.
I am the wallpaper / Mark Peter Hughes.
p. cm.
Summary: Thirteen-year-old Floey Packer, jealous of her attractive and popular older sister, shares her home with two younger cousins and experiences a summer vacation filled with embarrassing events, with herself as the star.
ISBN 978-0-385-73241-3 (trade) — ISBN 978-0-385-90265-6 (glb)
[1. Family life—Fiction. 2. Sibling rivalry—Fiction. 3. Cousins—Fiction. 4. Love—Fiction.] I. Title.
PZ7.H8736113Iae 2005
[Fic]—dc22
2004010163

ISBN 978-0-440-42046-0 (trade paperback)

Printed in the United States of America
10 9 8 7 6 5 4 3 2 1
First Readers Circle Edition

To Karen, *mi media naranja*

I'd like to thank Claudia Sorsby for her insights and suggestions, and Stephanie Lane, my editor, for sticking with me. I'm also indebted to the following people for their support: my parents, Suzanne Winnell Hughes and Peter Hughes; Carolyn Hughes Cuozzo; Jennifer Hughes; Luis Sasky; Mike Coco; Jennifer Fowler; Susan Green; Paul Griffiths; Dan Hillman; Mark Hurwitz; Janne Kaas; Thomas Gavin; Kevin McGurn; Paul Mullaney; Ann O'Rourke; Karen Rodgers; Sylvia Rogers; Jenny and Joel Silberman; Jane Williamson; and Ana and Leila Wons. Finally, special thanks go to my wife, Karen, for her love and encouragement, and to my wonderful children, Evan, Lucía, and Zoe.

i am the wallpaper

chapterone: in which i, floey packer, bust size 36b, receive a training bra or the cult of lillian

• • • • • • • • • • • •

I shouldn't have posed for the stupid photograph. True, Azra shouldn't have mailed it to Aunt Sarah, but if I hadn't stood there and let her take it in the first place my whole summer might have been completely different.

My thirteenth birthday, almost six months ago now, was the day everything really started: the spy club, what happened with Azra and Wen, the strange way I practically became famous. On that day back in March I had no clue what I was in for. How could I? At the time, the future looked perfect. This is what I wrote in my diary that morning:

Saturday, March 15, 10:00 a.m.

Finally, today I'm a teenager! I see the next year of my life waving me onward like Brad Pitt in a loincloth! Great things are about to happen. For example:

a. I will say goodbye to tech ed with Mr. Byrd. (Yay!)
b. I will say hello to eighth grade. (Hooray!)
c. Wendel will at long last admit that he likes me.*
d. Lillian will finally get a real job and move out of the house and I won't have to share a bedroom anymore.**

*This morning I thought of a plan to help him over his shyness thing—sort of a birthday gift from my brain! If I ask Gary, I'm pretty sure he'll give me a part-time job working with him and Wendel at the studio. Spending more time together ought to help the boy along. Sure, I'll need to figure out what to say to Azra, but as long as it's Wen who makes the move and not me, I haven't broken our deal, right? (Note to self: Start working up an interest in photography.)
**This, of course, may just be wishful thinking, but it's my birthday, so I can dream, can't I? (Note to self: Start leaving the Help Wanted section of the newspaper on Lillian's pillow.)

On top of all the other excitement of the day, I would also finally find out what was inside the mystery package from Aunt Sarah. A week before my birthday, it had arrived in the mail. That was kind of strange because I barely knew Aunt Sarah. Sure, I was aware that she lived in Chicago and that she was a teacher like my mom, but I hadn't seen her since my dad died, and that was when I was two. My mom was almost as curious as I was.

"So, are you going to open it now, Floey?"

"I can't," I said. "It says, 'Do not unwrap until March fifteenth.' "

So it sat on top of the television and I could only wonder what might be inside. It was kind of a fun mystery.

When my birthday finally came, Aunt Sarah's package sat at my feet along with a handful of other gift-wrapped boxes, waiting for me to reach down and open them. Five eager pairs of eyes looked on. Next to Azra, my best friend, sat Wen. He looked especially lovable in his new rectangular black-framed glasses. He still looked geeky, but in an artsy, hip kind of way. It was easy to see why Azra and I both had crushes on him. Near my mother sat Gary, my mother's tennis partner, and Frank Sinatra, my sister's crotchety old ferret. The only person missing was my sister, Lillian, who was already an hour late, typical for her. In fact, we'd just decided to go on without her.

But just as I was reaching for Aunt Sarah's package, Lillian showed up. Everyone turned to see her burst through the door with two complete strangers.

"Everybody, I'd like to introduce you to my new friends, Frida and Digger!" she said in her big, loud voice. "They're from Sweden!"

Frida and Digger were tall, smiling blond girls in giant parkas. They looked about the same age as Lillian, twenty-one. Lillian explained that she'd met them on the bus coming back from Providence, where she'd been walking some rich lady's dog.

She spoke slowly to the blonder of the two. "It *is* Digger, right?"

The other one, who must have been Frida, nodded. From the uncertain way the two girls looked at each other, I felt sure their English was shaky at best. Frida took out an unwrapped box of scented soaps. They'd obviously picked it out only moments earlier at the dollar store where the bus dropped them off.

"Happy birthday, Floey," Frida said to Azra, enunciating every syllable carefully and handing the box to my friend instead of me.

"Come on in," my mother said, sounding pleased that they were here to take over my birthday. "Let me take your coats. We were just getting started. Anybody want soda?"

That's when everybody, including Azra and Wen, stood up to say hello to my sister and her new friends, leaving me alone in my chair, the gift-wrapped boxes still unopened.

This was classic Lillian. My sister always had to be the bride at every wedding and the corpse at every funeral. She didn't care what she did to attract attention. Once, she climbed onto the roof of the town hall, saying she wouldn't come down until they stopped destroying the rain forests. Another time, when the school was thinking about starting a dress code, she showed up for her classes in a bikini. She was loud and rowdy and fun and everybody loved her for it. Of course, she was also thin and pretty, with thick dark hair and a perfect little nose, so boys practically burst their glands trying to get her to notice them.

She had about a zillion friends and all of them wanted to be just like her.

It was the Cult of Lillian.

Sometimes when my sister is around I feel almost invisible. I'm like the wallpaper, there but barely noticed. But this was especially frustrating because today was supposed to be *my* day, not hers.

Eventually, everyone settled back into the living room. Frida and Digger made themselves comfortable on the sofa between Azra and my mother while Lillian plopped down on the floor in front of Wen. Still, I was going to have to wait a little while longer to find out what was inside Aunt Sarah's package because now Lillian was entertaining everybody.

"Baba ghanoush," she said, dunking a celery stick into one of the dips my mother had laid out. "Don't you just love to say that? It practically flops around in your mouth. Baba ghanoush. Baba ghanoush."

Gary, whose comb-over looked particularly bizarre today (Ma said he was "losing" his hair, but as far as I could see he must have misplaced it long ago and there was no hope he'd ever find it again), sat back in the armchair and repeated it thoughtfully. "Baba ghanoush. Baba ghanoush." Then he chuckled. "You know, when you're right, you're right. It's a great word, Lil."

Soon, everybody was doing it. "Baba ghanoush. Baba ghanoush."

And nobody was paying any attention to me.

I am the wallpaper.

"Here, Floey," Wen said, finally breaking Lillian's spell. He was smiling and holding out a small square package wrapped in birthday paper. "This is for you."

Frida and Digger smiled politely.

As I unwrapped it, I had a feeling it might be the new Mudslide Crush CD. Happily, it was. "Thanks so much, Wen! I love it!"

Mudslide Crush is a cool local band. They record their own music and burn it to CD. Dean Eagler, the band's bass player and leader, is a tenth grader in my town, and every girl I know including Azra lusts after him, but I like Mudslide Crush because their stuff is great—kind of like garage music from outer space. They'd played our school Peace-A-Thon a few months before. Anyway, Wen and I are both into music. He plays the trumpet, so he knows a lot more about it than I do, but we like the same stuff. It was one of the reasons I knew we were perfect for each other.

"Floey," my mother said while I was still staring at the back cover, "why don't you open the one from Aunt Sarah?"

I set down the CD, finally ready for the mystery package. To open it, I had to peel away several layers of wrapping and then a few sheets of white tissue-paper filler. When I found the actual gift, I just stared at it.

"Come on, Floey," Lillian said. "What is it?"

Neatly folded at the bottom was a tiny pink bra.

By this time I'd been wearing real bras for almost a year, and I was much too big to fit into this one. I sprouted early, like Ma did. At school I hold my books in front of my chest so kids don't stare. It's really embarrassing. If Aunt Sarah had known anything at all about me, she'd have known this.

When Gary saw it, his whole head turned red. Everybody noticed. Lillian laughed and then so did Frida, Digger and Azra, and that made him turn even redder.

Wen saw it too. I nearly died.

"It's so small!" Lillian giggled. She held it up so everyone could see how ridiculous it was, and probably also to see how red Gary's face would get. Even Azra was too big for this—and Azra had no boobs at all.

"It's a training bra, hon," my mother said.

"That's stupid," I said, sure my cheeks were warm enough to fry eggs on. Imagine sending a bra to your niece! If I'd wanted another one, I'd have bought it myself. "What does she think I'm in training for?"

"Well, it's not the gift that matters." My mother snatched it out of Lillian's hands and packed it back into its box before the entire upper half of Gary's body could turn into a cherry. "It was sweet of her to remember your birthday, that's all. I want you to write her a nice thank-you note. Are you all right, Wen?"

"Yes, Mrs. Packer," Wen said, smiling his big goofy grin. "I'm just fine."

He had been looking at Azra, obviously pretending to be interested in something else rather than embarrass me by staring at the bra. That was my Wen, always so considerate!

• • •

Azra slept over that evening, so Lillian spent the night at her friend Rebecca's apartment. (At least, that's what she told my mother. I bet she really went to see Helmut, the latest and longest-running in her long line of adoring boyfriends.) In the bedroom, Azra, who was always coming up with stupid ideas, convinced me to try the bra on. I figured there wasn't any harm in it since there were only the two of us. I could barely strap the little thing around myself over my nightgown. We both thought it was hilarious. Frank Sinatra watched us from under my bed as if we were nuts. Then Azra took her Polaroid camera and told me to pose. Maybe if it hadn't been my birthday, if I hadn't been enjoying the rare attention, I wouldn't have agreed, but I did.

The picture was ridiculous. I was standing as if I were in a beauty pageant, my arms behind my head, staring coyly at a point somewhere above me. The tiny bra pushed my boobs up so all you could see in the V-neck of my nightgown was cleavage.

Azra and I nearly wet ourselves laughing.

Later, just before we went to sleep, Azra stared at my sister's graduation picture hanging over my stack of books. "You're so lucky," she said from Lillian's bed. She ran her fingers through her short black hair, which accentuated her long face. "Lillian is so great. I wish I had a sister like her."

"That's because you're an only child," I said. "Trust me, you don't."

"Why not? She's fabulous. She's one of the coolest people I know."

"Yeah, well, I wish she had an Off button."

"What do you mean? She's just wild and spontaneous. Didn't you think Frida and Digger were nice?"

"Sure," I said. "But you try living with Miss Wild and Spontaneous every day of your life."

"Oh, come on, Floey," Azra said, sitting up. "You're jealous."

"No, I'm not."

"You should try to be more like her."

I rolled my eyes.

Azra studied me, or at least she studied the top of my head from the nose up, the only part of me above the covers. "You know? I think I'm on to something. You're jealous because Lillian's glamorous and fun and popular and you're . . ."

I narrowed my eyes and waited.

". . . Well, you're you. You're just . . ."

"Ordinary?" I offered.

She shrugged. "I don't know . . . maybe."

I glowered at her. "Gee, thanks."

"That's not fair. You said it, not me. Anyway, I think you're great. And since we're best friends, I must be ordinary too, right?"

"Azra, you should go to sleep before I get really insulted."

I waited for her to get under her covers, but she just sat there for a while longer. "You know what our problem is?" she asked finally. "Low self-esteem."

"What?" Sometimes Azra is crazy.

"We *definitely* need to get boyfriends, and fast."

I didn't say anything. I was thinking about my plan to work at the studio with Wen. The thing was, it had been months since Azra and I had admitted to each other that we both had serious crushes on him. For both of us, it had started back in September on his first day at our school, the day they put him on our science lab team. We'd been a threesome from that day on. Since Azra and I had been best friends since second grade, we had agreed it would be best to share him and do nothing that might hurt our friendship. But it was obvious to me that I was the one Wen especially liked. We had the same weird sense of humor. Like, whenever he'd ask me what time it was, I'd answer, "You mean *now*?" Then, always with a straight face, he'd say something like, "Yes, but in Tokyo." We *got* each other. I figured he was practically my boyfriend already, he was just too shy to come out and say it. I was sure that my first-ever real kiss was only days away, at most. A part of me felt guilty about keeping these thoughts from Azra. It was the first secret I'd *ever* kept from her. If only we hadn't made that pact.

Of course, our deal didn't mean I couldn't spend a little extra time with him.

"You know what we should do?" Azra said, her voice suddenly more serious. "Something wild and adventurous, like Lillian would do. Something the ordinary you and me would never do in a million years. It'd be good for us."

"Like what?"

She frowned. "I don't know. Maybe get belly-button rings?"

"Don't hold your breath."

"Stand naked in front of the school and make speeches?"

I laughed. "Too cold. And public speaking makes me break out."

"I know what *you* could do," she said. "Why don't you send that picture of you in that bra to your aunt? That'd get her attention."

I gave her a not-in-a-trillion-years look and turned out the light.

"Good night."

I heard her rustling around under her covers. Eventually, after everything was quiet, she said, "You should do it. You really should."

I laughed.

I didn't laugh the next night, though, when Azra called to tell me she'd put the picture in a thank-you note and dropped it in the mail. She'd copied the address off the birthday package and had written and signed a card as if it were from me.

"You did *what*?"

"Dear Aunt Sarah," she said, giggling. "Thank you for the lovely training bra. It was sweet of you to remember my birthday. P.S. It's just what I need, now that I'm in training."

"You didn't!"

"I knew you wouldn't do it yourself—you think too much about everything. So I had to do it for you. It's the first step toward breaking us out of our shells. Floey

Packer, you have now broken free from your ordinary, drab little world."

For an otherwise sensible girl, Azra had some stupid ideas. I wondered if somebody dropped her on her head as a baby.

She giggled again.

Ha ha.

I didn't speak to her for two weeks. Even after that, it took us a while to get beyond this. But after she slipped a tin of homemade peanut butter brownies, my favorite, into my backpack, I was able to remind myself that, misguided as she was, she was my best friend and she meant well.

• • •

I should have called Aunt Sarah right away to tell her that the thank-you note wasn't from me, but I didn't want to think about it—it was just too horrible. And then time went by. By the time Lillian announced her engagement to Helmut and I realized I was actually going to have to see Aunt Sarah at the wedding—and found out that her two kids would be staying with us for the three weeks after the wedding—it was too late.

After that, in the months leading up to the big event, I blushed every time I thought of my aunt.

chaptertwo: in which my sister gets married or dodging aunt sarah

• • • • • • • • • • • •

Saturday, June 28, 7:10 a.m.

I am too depressed for words. My sister is getting married today, so I should be enjoying myself, but the following things are ruining it for me:

a. Wen dumped me.
b. It's clear to me now that he never had any idea he was my boyfriend.
c. The wedding is going ahead even though I have convincing evidence that love doesn't last and only ends in pain. (See item a.)
d. For the next three weeks there will be two strange kids, cousins I barely know, in my home, my personal space. Worse, one of them will share my room.
e. If I don't find a way to avoid Aunt Sarah today, I may just die of shame.
f. Frank Sinatra has been looking at me like I'm out of my mind.
g. He might be right.

Thank God Rebecca Greenblatt was such a fatty.

Rebecca, the other bridesmaid, shifted her position, so I shifted mine, too. She was chunky enough that if I kept behind her, I could stay pretty well hidden from about a third of the guests, including Aunt Sarah.

From the front row of folding chairs, my mother was giving me the evil eye. *Floey,* she mouthed silently, *stop . . . moving.*

I fixed my gaze on the main event and pretended not to see her.

With her veil, tiara and bouquet of white lilies, Lillian looked like a princess. I, on the other hand, clutching my Alice-in-Wonderland bouquet (What flower has big, red, floppy elephant-ear petals? And who, other than my sister, would choose them for her wedding?), felt ridiculous in my bridesmaid gown. It was a horrible pink thing with ruffles and a silly neck, and it looked even worse on than it did hanging in my closet. Anyone who wore this dress should have been blond and waiflike, and I was neither. I felt like a troll in a doily.

Seeing how happy Lillian and Helmut looked only made me consider how pointless relationships were. I've read that half of all marriages end in divorce. Doesn't that tell you something? In Ma's case it wasn't divorce, but I bet when she got married, she never thought her husband would just drop dead and leave her with two daughters, aged ten and two, to raise by herself. Sure, Helmut and Lillian seemed happy now, but how long could it last?

Then, of course, there was Wen and me.

For almost three months we'd been working together part-time as Gary's assistants, going every few days to the photography studio, helping at the front desk and getting the cameras and backgrounds ready. Wen was funny and sweet with me, and eventually I started thinking of us as kind of a unit. At home I talked about him so much that my mother and Lillian asked if he was my boyfriend, and stupidly, I told them he was. At the time, I didn't think it was a big leap. I thought of him as *practically* my boyfriend already.

Only I never told him.

I know that sounds dumb, but I didn't. I guess I didn't want him to tell me it wasn't true.

And then the bomb dropped. Three days before the wedding, Wen quit the studio, supposedly so he could spend more time on his music. Later that day, Azra saw him holding hands with Kim Swift. Only then did I realize that, incredibly, Wen had no idea how I felt about him. If I hadn't already been convinced I was invisible, that was all the proof I would have needed.

I never told my mother or Lillian. What would I have said? That I was dumped from a relationship that had never really existed in the first place? I was too embarrassed.

As I watched Lillian take her vows, I wondered if Wen and Kim were together now, not thinking about me.

Oh God! Would I ever be able to stop torturing myself?

Gary was standing between the minister and the harpist, taking pictures. Every now and then I caught him taking his eye off the wedding to sneak a look at my mother. I was pretty sure he had a thing for her. Between snapping shots and stealing peeks at Ma, he kept wiping tears from his eyes. Gary's a big crier. For his sake and for the sake of the wedding album, I hoped he'd make it through the ceremony without melting away.

"Lillian, do you take Helmut to be your husband, to love, honor and comfort, to keep in sickness and in health, forsaking all others, from this day forward, so long as you both shall live?"

That's when I felt the first raindrop on my nose. A moment later another big fat blob plopped on my ear, dribbled down my neck and eventually soaked itself into the poofy pink shoulder of my awful dress. My mother's face suddenly looked panicky. Some of the guests glanced up at the sky.

If everyone was forced inside, where was I going to hide?

Soon the wind picked up and my elephant-ear bouquet flapped around. Then, all at once, the raindrops began to fall more quickly and the minister started talking a lot faster. By the time the wedding party hurried up the aisle with the guests hurling birdseed, my dress was almost soaked.

"The flowers!" Lillian wailed.

"Everybody grab something!" my mother shouted.

Friends and relatives grabbed the giant arrangements of bizarre flowers and hustled them, along with anything else that seemed important, up the back steps and inside to safety. Our house wasn't really big enough for seventy-two people. Other than our big living room, there were only the two bedrooms, the kitchen, a small television room, and a tiny office the size of a closet. Still, there was no choice except to cram everybody in.

Lillian was so upset by the unexpected rain that she locked herself in our only bathroom, crying. Her new husband stood at the door trying to comfort her for twenty minutes before she finally agreed to come out and rejoin her guests, who flocked around her sympathetically.

I, on the other hand, found an empty corner and sat there quietly for at least half an hour. In such a small house, staying out of sight would have been difficult for anybody else. But not for me.

Right then, for instance, my mother was standing only a few feet from me, talking with Gary and poor Helmut's square-faced father, but I could tell she had no idea I was there.

Wallpaper, thy name is Floey.

For ten minutes, I'd been sitting so close to Ma that I could almost have reached my arm out and touched her. Would she ever look in my direction? How could she not notice me?

A tray of champagne glasses drifted by. My mother always made a big deal that she didn't want me drinking alcohol, so as a test, I stood up and grabbed one of the glasses. "Hello, Ma," I said through the wall of people. "I'm right here and I have a glass of champagne."

She kept talking.

I decided to wave my arms around, moving the glass

back and forth in front of my face, trying to get her attention. Incredibly, she still didn't notice me. I felt like Molly Ringwald in *Sixteen Candles*. No, worse. At least at the end of the movie, the forgotten girl gets the cute guy in the red car. Where was my cute guy in the red car?

Then my glass knocked into something hard. It was a blue suit.

"Whoops! Hold on!" it said.

"Oh, I'm so sorry! I didn't—"

The boy in the suit took out a handkerchief and wiped his jacket, which now had a dark wet streak on one sleeve. He was older, fifteenish.

"It's all right, it's all right," he said in a slow, friendly voice.

"Really, I feel just horrible!" I grabbed a couple of napkins from the sideboard next to me and tried to help him.

"No, no. It's fine." He had a slight accent like he was from the South or something, definitely not from Rhode Island. "It's not so bad. That's why they make them with two arms."

I stopped wiping. He was smiling at me. He was a head taller than me, blond, with the bluest eyes I'd ever seen.

"Have you been standing here all on your own?" he asked.

I shrugged.

"Listen, I do believe we ought to get you another glass of champagne." At that moment the tray came by again, so he grabbed two glasses and held one out for me.

"No, thank you. That other one was just for show. My mother doesn't allow it."

He stepped in a little closer. "I wouldn't worry about that," he said, still holding out the drink. "What your mother doesn't know won't hurt her."

"But my mother *would* know. She'd see." I nodded toward where Ma stood.

When he saw who she was, he stepped back a little. "You couldn't be . . . you're not Lillian's little eleven-year-old sister, are you?"

I shook my head. "Thirteen."

"Oh, I'm sorry," he said, blushing. "I didn't know. I guess I should have—You look a lot like her."

I probably ought to have been flattered, but beyond the dark wavy hair and pale skin, I think we only look alike if you're not paying attention. Still, he seemed so nice I didn't want to argue.

"It's just that you seem older than I expected. More, you know, mature." I didn't want him to see how happy that made me, so I tried my best to keep a poker face. He looked down at the chair I'd been sitting in and then glanced around at the crowded room. "It must be hard for you today."

I studied his beautiful face. Was he only being nice to me because he thought I was just a sad nobody who needed cheering up, or did he really think I was mature? I wished I weren't wearing the Glinda the Good Witch costume.

My mother was still listening to the square-faced man, only now his jolly-looking wife had joined them. Here I was just a few feet away with an older boy who might even have lewd intentions, and Ma was completely oblivious.

"I changed my mind," I said. "I *will* have that champagne."

He hesitated, but I grabbed the glass out of his hand and took a sip. It was sweet, like lemon soda.

"Maybe we'd better go into the kitchen," he said. "Would you like to come with me?"

I almost said no, but he moved away, so I followed him. We had to fight our way through the people. Once we reached the kitchen, a group of Helmut's incredibly tall, German-speaking relatives blocked us from my mother's view. We found an empty space at the corner of the counter.

"Okay, she's not around anymore." He raised his glass. "To never being afraid to have a glass of champagne at your own sister's wedding."

I felt my cheeks grow warm. I raised my glass too and then emptied it in one long swallow. He watched me, surprised. Finally, I handed him the empty glass and said, "What's your name?"

"I'm Calvin," he laughed. "Helmut's uncle, sort of. His stepmother is my sister."

Another failed relationship.

"I like your accent," I said. "Where are you from?"

"Providence," he said, and then grinned. "But transplanted two years ago from Oklahoma City."

"I'm Floey," I said. Then I noticed the top of Aunt Sarah's head bobbing in the doorway of the television room just above one of the shorter German ladies. "Would you mind standing right here?"

Since Calvin didn't seem to understand and wasn't moving quickly enough, I grabbed him by the arms and pulled him into place. I was starting to feel a comfortable glow across my face.

"Wh-what?"

I whispered into his ear. "It's my aunt Sarah. I don't want to talk to her."

"Ahh . . . ," he said, as if he understood. He looked over his shoulder. "Which one is she?"

"Skinny lady. Tight hairdo. Ugly brown dress. Please don't stare." He turned back. He had a wonderful smile. I suddenly felt relaxed and wicked. "What do you do when you're not pushing alcoholic beverages on underage girls?"

He grinned. "I'm a poet." When I didn't say anything, he continued, "Well, I go to school, of course. Moses Brown. I'll be a sophomore this September. But I do poetry readings all the time. You know, open-mike nights."

I liked the idea that I was talking with a handsome, soulful artist from Oklahoma. And a high school sophomore. Hmmmm. Very exciting.

"You stand in front of people and read poems? I couldn't do that."

"Sure you could," he said. "An audience can bring out the best in a person. It's fun, too."

"No, I really couldn't. The last time I had to give an oral report in class I nearly passed out. They sent me to the nurse."

"You putting me on?"

I shook my head.

He seemed to consider this for a moment. "I guess I used to be kind of the same way," he said. "Whenever I had to give any kind of speech or whatever at school, I couldn't sleep the night before. The first time I read one of my poems to an audience, I pretty much had to force myself. But after a few times, I got over it. It doesn't bother me now."

I stared at him. "Sounds like torture to me."

He looked like he didn't know what to say, so I changed the subject. "What does that mean?" I asked, pointing at the little round pin on his shirt pocket. It said LIFE IS SUFFERING, ZEN YOU DIE.

"This?" he said, looking down at it. "Oh, it's sort of a Buddhist thing. Deep, don't you think?" He must have seen that I was still puzzled because then he said, "Maybe it's about how insignificant we all are, compared to the universe and all that. Know what I mean?"

"Sort of depressing."

He shrugged. "Can I move my head now?"

"Oh, I'm sorry," I said, looking carefully over his shoulder. "Yes, I think she's gone."

He turned his head but there was nothing to see except dressed-up people squished together like pickles in a jar. He laughed. "You're a very . . . interesting person, Floey Packer."

This time I couldn't help grinning.

"So," he said. "What do you do when you're not hiding from your relatives?"

I started giggling and then so did he. It surprised me that I felt so comfortable talking with this complete stranger, this Adonis. It was the first relaxed moment I'd had all day. I was just about to ask him if he was really a Buddhist when my mother's voice rose above the other noise.

"The caterer is ready to serve dinner," she said, sounding almost like she was apologizing. I caught a flash of her purple dress between two giant German men standing in the doorway. "It's going to be a little crowded, and we'll need help setting up the tables."

I looked back into Calvin's blue, blue eyes and suddenly found myself unable to speak. I didn't want our conversation to end. So far he had been the one cheerful part of an almost completely cheer-free weekend.

He gave me another friendly smile and squeezed my arm as if to say, "Don't worry. You are by far the best thing at this wedding. Everything will be all right." What he actually said was, "Well, I guess it's time to help out. Catch you later."

And then he left and I was alone again.

Maybe it was the champagne starting to affect me, but instead of feeling abandoned I felt strangely excited. Out of all the people here, this nice, incredibly gorgeous poet had chosen to talk with me, Floey. And even though he'd gone away, he had said "Catch you later," hadn't he? And didn't that mean he wanted to talk even more?

• • •

Folding tables sprang up in just about every available space: not only in the living room, but also in each of the bedrooms and even some in the doorways between rooms. Eventually, my mother and Lillian came to get me.

"There you are," my mother said, taking my arm. "Let me walk you to your table. Come with me."

They brought me to my own bedroom. Somebody had moved my desk to make room for a small card table, where all the little children, none of them over eleven and a few of them much younger, were sitting. They grinned at me.

I was horrified.

"Ma, you're not serious! I don't want to eat here, with *them*."

"I'm sorry, honey. Please don't make a fuss." She tugged at an unraveling curl. "I'm afraid it's the only spot we have."

"I'm not a child. I don't belong at this table. If this is the only place for me then I'll eat standing up. Or I won't eat at all!"

Lillian's eyes welled up with fresh tears. "Floey always has to ruin everything for me, Ma! This is my wedding, and I want her to eat at a table!"

"We don't have time for a scene, Floey. Why don't you just do it? This one day, please be flexible."

I took a deep breath and counted to ten. I didn't want to make a fuss because I knew I'd never ever hear the end of it. In twenty years, Lillian would probably still tell the story of how I wrecked her wedding day. It was better just to go along with them. Besides, by now I was feeling kind of funny and light-headed from the champagne, so I didn't want to fight.

I sat down at the table, crossed my arms and glared at Lillian.

"Thank you, Floey," my mother said. "That was very adult of you. The caterer will bring the food soon. It won't be so bad." She gave me a sympathetic look, and then she and Lillian left to join the other guests.

The sounds of toasting and celebrating reached us from all the way across the house. I hoped Calvin wouldn't see me back here.

I sipped at the lobster bisque in silence, trying to ignore the children. Aunt Sarah's two kids, Richard and Tish, were at the table. This was the first time all day that I'd come face to face with them. Even though they were my cousins, I didn't really know them. The only time we'd ever met was when I was six and they were four and three. Since I'd been steering clear of my aunt all afternoon, I'd also managed to avoid them. Still, they were going to stay with us for three whole weeks, so I couldn't avoid them forever.

While the other kids talked and laughed with each other, the younger one, Tish, just stared at me. She was ten years old and a real porker. "Is this your room?" she asked finally.

The other children stopped their conversations and turned to listen.

"That's right," I said, uncomfortable with everyone gawking at me.

She nodded, glancing around the room. It was hard to tell where her chin ended and her neck began. The girl was an absolute jelly roll.

"How come you're hardly eating?" asked a little girl with a missing tooth. "Are you on a diet?"

I still felt a little giddy. "What's it to you?"

She shrugged.

"Know what happens to nosy little girls? The tooth fairy comes in the middle of the night and chops their little heads off, that's what. So mind your own business."

The little girl laughed and then so did all the other children. "You're funny," she said.

That's when Tish reached under the table to her lap and pulled up a photograph. "Who's this?" she asked.

I nearly choked. She was holding up a picture of Wen.

"Hey! Give me that!" It was the picture I'd been keeping next to my clock radio—until two nights before, when I'd hurled it into the trash. The little horror must have fished it out!

She looked hurt but handed the photo to me. "Is he your boyfriend?"

"It's none of your business!"

"I think he is. Look, he's the same boy in that picture over there."

Everybody turned. She was pointing to the photograph of Wen and Azra and me at the Halloween dance the past October. Wen stood in the middle, laughing behind sunglasses and fake whiskers with his arms across both of our shoulders. We were the three blind mice.

I glared at her. "You don't know anything about me."

After another uncomfortable silence, I looked down at my lemon chicken and summer vegetables, trying to pretend I was alone in the room.

The big lump across the table from me shifted in his chair. His name was Billy Fishman and he lived next door. Even though he was only eleven, he was already huge, almost mutant-sized. He looked like a side of roast beef with a clip-on tie.

"I know something about you," he said in a voice surprisingly high and squeaky for such a gorilla.

I waited.

He leaned forward, eyes narrowed. "You go to bed late. You read before you go to sleep. You read a *lot*."

"That's right," I said, surprised. "How do you know that?"

He looked smug. "I know."

"How?"

"Easy. My bedroom is right there." He pointed to one of my windows, the one that looked directly across the lawn to his house.

"So you've been *watching* me?"

He smiled.

I didn't know what to say. I was totally freaked out. I tried to think when he might have seen me and what he might have seen. But there was nothing I could do now. One thing was for sure: in the future I was definitely going to be more careful about lowering the shade.

I went back to eating.

But then Richard said, "I know something else about you." Unlike his sister, Richard was small, pale and spooky-looking, with bushy brown hair that fell over his eyes. Ma had told me he was having some problems at school and that he didn't have many friends. Apparently, he'd won some prize at school, something to do with computers. That was all I needed—three weeks with a computer geek.

I kept eating.

"My mother was talking about you. She said I should watch out for you. She said you're not an especially nice young lady."

Something in my stomach turned sour. "What?" I asked, looking up from my plate. "Why would she say that?"

He had a sly, devilish grin. "You know why." He went back to his food without explaining further. He hummed as he cut a bite of chicken and ate it. After he took two more mouthfuls, I was still glaring at him, so he looked over and grinned again. "It was because of that picture you sent," he said. "You know, the birthday picture."

I was suddenly gladder than ever that I'd been avoiding my aunt.

"Why is your face turning red?" another kid asked.

Richard laughed. "I know why. She's embarrassed, that's why. And she should be."

"You never saw that picture," I said, even though I wasn't sure.

He shrugged. "Maybe, maybe not."

I wanted to run out of the room, but that would only

make the kids laugh more, so I controlled myself and tried, once again, to concentrate on my food. But before I could bring a single carrot up to my mouth, something hit me in the face. I looked down at the tablecloth. It was a cube of cheese.

The little girl with the missing tooth giggled.

I put down my fork and knife. One after another, I threw five cherry tomatoes at her. The demonic child only giggled more.

Richard tapped me on the shoulder. He motioned for me to put my ear to his mouth so he could tell me a secret. I don't know why I did it, but I did.

"Nice titties," he whispered. He posed his arms and face the same exact way I had done in the picture. I couldn't believe it.

When he started to laugh, I didn't know what else to do, so I picked up the rest of my salad and threw it at him. He ducked, so most of it missed him. And then he just laughed and picked off the few pieces of lettuce and cucumber that had hit his shirt. Why had I let Azra take that picture? What had I been thinking?

I stood up and left the room, my face probably turning the color of one of Lillian's elephant-ear wedding flowers. A group of my sister's friends stood in line in front of the bathroom. Even after I pushed my way through them I could still hear the children laughing.

I searched for Calvin and found him sitting at one of the tables in the living room. Everybody was laughing and having a nice time. I wished I could have sat there with them. If only I could go back in time to the morning of my birthday, when everything still seemed wonderful.

Behind the happy people eating at their tables, the rain flooded down the living room bay window, distorting everything into slowly twisting blue and green tentacles, as if a huge octopus held me trapped inside the house.

Suddenly, I found myself face to face with Aunt Sarah.

chapterthree: in which i dance, sort of, and make a huge decision

• • • • • • • • • • • •

"*There* you are, darling," Aunt Sarah said. Her deep voice surprised me almost as much as running into her did. She smiled, but she didn't look friendly. "I was wondering if we were ever going to get a chance to . . . catch up."

I looked around frantically for some way to escape, but it was no use.

"Oh, hello, Aunt Sarah," I managed.

"Hello indeed. I hope you've been keeping yourself out of trouble. Have you?"

"I guess so." I tried to come up with something else to say, but I had a hard time thinking about anything other than that stupid picture. "Aunt Sarah," I said. "I'm sorry. About, you know, the thank-you card."

"Thank-you card? Oh, that. Yes. Well. It certainly was . . . unexpected."

"I know," I said, looking at my shoes. "It was kind of rude."

"Yes, it certainly was. Rude and ignorant. Decidedly ungrateful, too. Do you have any idea how disrespectful it was? You should just be thankful I never told your mother about it."

This wasn't going well.

"When I was your age I would never have dreamt of sending a . . . an *insult* like that. But I suppose times have changed."

"Aunt Sarah," I said, "you should know that it wasn't actually me who sent that card. It was my friend Azra."

She snorted, obviously not believing me.

Suddenly the bathroom door opened and Gary appeared next to us. Thank God. I caught his eye and flashed him a please-save-me look. He glanced from me to Sarah and then gave us both a warm smile.

"Floey!" he said. "Just the person I've been looking for. We need your help clearing up the tables to make room for dancing." He turned to Aunt Sarah. "I'm sorry, but I'm afraid I'm going to have to steal her away from you."

Thank you, Gary.

• • •

But my encounter with Aunt Sarah wasn't even the most terrible part of the day. The most terrible part happened during the dancing.

The DJ had set up the sound system in a corner of the living room, but you could hear the music all over the house. Unfortunately, he played Louis Armstrong, the famous trumpet player, and that reminded me of Wen.

I needed to get away from all the dancing couples.

I found myself a relatively isolated sofa in the television

room. Some of Helmut's German relatives were there, but since their conversations were in German I didn't need to join in.

A short gray tail stuck out from behind a chair. Like me, Frank Sinatra wanted everyone to go away. I knew this because he *always* wanted everyone to go away. He was a horribly unsociable ferret. He'd hiss whenever anybody came too near him, even Lillian. Anybody except me. For whatever reason (probably because I was the only one who fed him or emptied his litter box), I seemed to be the human he disliked the least. He sat on me sometimes, and let me stroke his fur when it suited him. Anyway, we both wanted to be alone. In that way, we were like soul mates.

Except, as I say, he didn't exactly like me.

I listened to the babbling of German voices over the old-fashioned music. I'd just finished my second glass of champagne and started another when I began feeling like I was fading into the pattern of gold leaves on the wall behind me.

That's when Calvin came into the room.

Actually, I'm not sure exactly when he came in or how long he'd been standing nearby, because I'd been daydreaming. Gradually, though, I realized that the room wasn't nearly as full of people as before. Almost all of the Germans had left to go into the living room for the dancing. Calvin was talking with the last one, a curly-haired tree with a mustache. I reached out and touched Calvin's leg.

"Calvin?"

"Whoa, hey!" he said, turning around. But then he saw

me. "Floey? Hi! I didn't see you there. You sure are a quiet one, aren't you?"

I smiled. We were finally going to chat again.

"So," he began, "where did they end up fitting you in?"

"Don't ask," I said, happy that he seemed glad to see me. With the warm glow from the champagne, I couldn't help giggling a little. I felt more comfortable now. I decided I loved a boy in a blue double-breasted suit and floral tie.

I stood up. The curly-haired tree left us without a word.

Right then one of the peppier songs ended and a slow, romantic one began. I didn't know this one, but I liked it.

I worked up my courage. "Want to dance?"

"Uh, I'm not a very good dancer," he said.

"Oh, come on. I can show you." I stepped closer, and before I even realized I'd done it, I'd taken his hand. Even at the time I could hardly believe it. I'd never in my entire life been so daring with a boy, especially not a cute one like Calvin. But for some reason the normal, cautious me seemed to have disappeared, or at least faded a little. It must have been the champagne.

"Here? But I'm not . . ." And he blushed, which made me *very* happy.

Since I'd already gone this far, I figured I might as well keep going. "It's a slow song. You don't really need to know how to dance when it's a slow song. I'll show you." Trying my best to act casual, I put my arms around his shoulders. Amazingly, he didn't stop me. In fact, he put his hands uncertainly around me and rested them against my back.

"That's good," I said, my heart beating through my chest. "Now sway."

We started rocking back and forth. His rhythm was good, but his movements were a little stiff. He looked as unsure as I felt.

"You're doing great," I said, still trying to seem like this was normal for me. "But you have to relax. We're just moving with the music. That's all there is to it."

A moment later he seemed to get it. His body, loosened up a little now, felt warm, and his blue, blue eyes gazed down into mine. It was nice. I'd danced with boys at school dances, but this felt entirely different, and much more exciting. I felt like we were under some magical spell. After a while, I even found the courage to rest my head on his chest.

But then he said, "Floey, is this really a good idea? You're only thirteen and I'm fift—"

"Shhhh." I cut him off. A part of me—the new, crazy, unrealistic part I'd never known was there before—didn't want to break the spell. So he was a couple of years older—what did that matter? We were moving back and forth, back and forth. This was very nice. The music, Calvin's arms around me and the champagne making me feel just . . . perfect. But I guess the champagne must have affected my judgment even more than I'd realized, because that's when I suddenly got the wildest idea of all.

I decided I was going to kiss him.

Sure, there was still that faint, cautious voice that said this was crazy, but as soon as that idea entered my head, I shoved it right back out again. I knew that if I thought about it too much I'd never kiss him, so I'd better do it right away. I leaned forward to bring my lips closer to his.

But then another unexpected thing happened.

We both screamed.

He'd lost his balance and so had I. Somehow, I must have pushed him backward and knocked him into the coffee table. The next thing I knew we were on our sides, our bodies tangled together, half on the table, half on the sofa. His arm was trapped under my shoulder and mine was pinned under him.

"Oh my God," I said. "I'm so sorry! Are you okay?"

He nodded but didn't say anything. He was staring at my face.

That's when I realized that my hand was pressed firmly into his butt.

Suddenly the fuzzy glow from the champagne was gone. I was mortified. I tried to untangle myself, but he was heavy.

And then I heard Lillian's voice.

"Floey? What are you *doing*?"

Calvin and I both spun our heads to face the door. Lillian stood there, her veil hanging lopsided from her head, and pop-eyed behind her were Rebecca Greenblatt and Aunt Sarah. Everyone stared.

"Now *there's* a picture for the wedding album," Lillian said.

I yanked my hand away and pulled myself off him. I

couldn't bear to imagine what everybody was thinking as Calvin and I stood up and straightened ourselves out.

"This isn't what it looks like . . . ," I tried to explain, but I could see they weren't buying it. In waves, the happiness from just a few moments ago died away, and all of a sudden I wanted to barf.

Rebecca laughed.

Lillian shook her head slowly. "You better hope Wen never finds out about this, Floey. Ma either."

Head down, Calvin quickly stepped past me and pushed through Lillian, Rebecca and Aunt Sarah, leaving me alone with them. I wondered how much more it would take for me to just shrivel up and disappear.

Rebecca laughed so hard she had to hold on to the doorframe.

I lowered my face, covered my eyes with my hand and pressed past them toward the bathroom, where I hoped to stay until the end of this God-awful day. No matter what I did for the rest of my life, I knew I'd never be able to get past the shame I felt at this moment.

When I finally reached the door, it was locked, so I ran to my bedroom. My cousins were gone; the room was empty. I slammed the door. Finally alone, I leaned against the door, closed my eyes and decided to stay in my room until the last guest left.

In the big room, the dancing continued.

Soon, though, I heard those awful kids pounding back down the hallway, laughing and playing. They knocked on the door.

"Open up!" one of them shouted.

"Go away!"

They pushed against the door, so I pushed back. But there were too many of them. As hard as I pushed, I couldn't stop them from moving the door just enough to let one of the little girls through.

"What's the matter with you?" she said. "You can't take a whole room!"

"This is my room, so get out." I kept my back against the door.

The little girl shook her head. "Your mother said that today this is *our* room." She grabbed my arm and tried to pull me away. The other children shouted and kicked the door. The music and laughter from the living room were louder now.

"Let them in, room hog!" the little girl screamed. She kicked me in the shin. I grabbed my leg, and the other children finally tumbled in and the room filled up with little kids again.

"Get her out!" the girl shouted, and soon all the children were chanting it over and over, grabbing my arms and pulling me out of the room. "Get her out! Get her out!" It was like a nightmare. The children opened the door to the back steps, just outside my room. I kicked and shouted, but I couldn't stop them.

"Get her out! Get her out!"

They forced me outside. Then the door slammed in my face.

The small wooden shelter over the top step wasn't

enough to protect me from the wind and the rain. I tried the handle but the children had locked it. "Open up!" I pounded on the door. Through the window I saw them laughing at me. My cousin Richard yanked down the shade.

Suddenly all I could see was gray.

It only took a few more seconds for my dress and hair to get soaked through. I stared at the shade until water dribbled from my bangs and down my face. I closed my eyes. Was there any point in going back inside?

The rain slapped against the roof. My dress was already cold and heavy.

Life is suffering, Zen you die.

I now believe that there are some moments so life-changing that your mind remembers them with almost superhuman clarity, as if everything is running in slow motion. For me, this was one of those Pivotal Life Moments. I was tired of being taken advantage of. I was sick of being unnoticed, unimportant, powerless and invisible. I could almost see myself, standing in front of the door, drenched and dripping. It was like I was my future self watching my present-day self from the outside, listening to her think.

It was really Zen.

All at once I understood that this moment could only be bearable if I made it the beginning of a new era in my life. If I went back inside, things would have to change. I felt my future self watching me, waiting for my next decision.

I needed to consider my next move carefully, so I stood in the rain for a while.

Eventually, I turned around and slowly and deliberately slogged down the back steps and around the side of the house. As my bubblegum pink shoes squelched through the mud, I made my decision.

This is what I wrote in my diary that night:

Sunday, June 29, 1:00 a.m.

To the older, wiser me,

You probably still remember this awful day pretty clearly. As of right now my friends and family hardly notice me, or they laugh at me or hate me because they don't know me. But I have some news for them: the days of the invisible, ordinary, wallpaper Floey Packer are over. Tonight marks the birth of a whole new me.

One other important note for the future: I will never drink champagne again. Ever.

I trudged up the long brick stairway to the front door and grasped the handle. The music was still loud enough that I could feel the vibrations through the metal. I took one extra moment to gather my courage, but then I opened the door and stepped inside.

A whole room full of family and strangers turned to look at the crazy wet girl dripping in the doorway. Even the music paused between songs, almost as though it knew I'd come in. For a few seconds, the party screeched to a halt as everybody noticed me, my sopping wet dress, my shoes covered in mud, my hair flat against my head. They didn't know it, but my future self, a bold, remarkable new Floey, had arrived.

Nothing would ever be the same again.

chapterfour: in which children from hell move into my house and interrupt a life-changing personal transformation

• • • • • • • • • • • •

I didn't see Calvin again that evening. He left and never came back. This is what I wrote in my diary the next morning:

Sunday, June 29, 8:00 a.m.

Dear Future Floey,

Calvin is the only one who truly appreciates me. I will find him again even if it means I have to search every class at Moses Brown and every open-mike poetry night in Rhode Island.

But first I had a few little obstacles to take care of.

Since Aunt Sarah's support group for divorced mothers had signed up for a three-week Alaskan adventure—supposedly to learn something about themselves—we had to transform our house so we could take her kids. Ma said it'd be good for me to get to know my cousins better. "It'll be fun," she said, "like being at summer camp."

Ha.

The summer-camp preparations began with my dear mother making me wash the windows, vacuum up the ferret hair and scrub the toilet. Craziest of all, she was going to force me to clean my cousins' bedrooms (meaning my room and the TV room) *every day*! I understood making me take care of my own stuff, but why should I have to clean up after them, too? I could point out the obvious unfairness of this until my tongue wore out, but it wouldn't make any difference. Richard and Tish were going to be our guests, Ma said. If this was a summer camp, I was the camp cleaning lady.

There is no justice.

When we were done cleaning, I had to think of a way out of going with Ma to pick up Aunt Sarah and my cousins at their hotel, shuttling them up to Logan Airport in time for Aunt Sarah's flight and then ferrying the kids back here to start their three-week stay with us. Fortunately, the New Floey Packer was a take-charge kind of girl. Unlike the Old Floey, she wasn't going to let life just happen around her.

"Can't," I told Ma. "I'm having cramps. Very bad cramps." This was a trick of Lillian's. Tried and true.

A couple of minutes later Ma produced two ibuprofen pills and a glass of water and set them next to my bed. "I called Gary," she said. "He'll drive into Boston with me."

"He will? That's almost three hours round-trip. He agreed to that pretty quick."

She shrugged and gave me an innocent smile.

Gary sure was trying hard. You had to feel sorry for him. My mother hadn't dated anybody since my dad died. She'd told Lillian and me that she probably never would, and that even if she did it would only be after we both grew up and moved away. Poor Gary.

Anyway, as soon as the door closed, I went to the computer in the little office off the kitchen. The minute I sat down, Frank Sinatra stopped running around in neurotic circles and flung himself into my lap. He was a ferret with social issues but good taste.

Since it was summer, there was no point in looking up the English department at Moses Brown. Instead, I searched for poetry readings. I typed *open-mike poetry* and got 150,000 hits. Even when I refined my search to *Rhode Island open-mike poetry*, there were still too many to be useful.

So after a few futile minutes I gave up and typed *Zen*.

There was another long list of Web sites. I clicked on one of them at random. At the top of the screen was the title *Zen Thought of the Day*. Today's thought was: *What is the sound of one hand clapping?*

There was no answer, just the question. I stared at it for a few seconds. I had no idea what it was supposed to mean.

Below the thought of the day was a poem:

nothing in the cry
of cicadas suggests they
are about to die

—Matsuo Basho 1644-1694

Five seven five. Haiku.

Did Calvin write haiku? Probably. That inspired me to make up two of my own:

Sunday, June 29, 10:20 a.m.

alone in the house
unseen among the shadows
today i'm all new

so long aunt sarah
fly far far away from your
rude ignorant niece

Would the future Floey Packer be a famous poet? I pictured myself spending hours alone in beautiful fields thinking deep, inspired thoughts. Then, concentrating again on the computer, I clicked on a few other links at random and printed out the pages so I could bring them to my room and read them. But as soon as I sat on my bed the doorbell rang.

Sunday, June 29, 11:10 a.m.

That was Azra. She wanted us to go to the secret beach but I have too much going on, so we stayed here. Here are the updates:

1. Leslie Dern has apparently become the center of Azra's universe. Azra's all excited about being a

YMCA day-camp junior counselor this summer, and I guess she found out at training yesterday that Leslie's doing it too. I'm irked that she signed up without me. It wasn't my fault Lillian put her wedding on the exact same day as JC training! Suddenly everything with Azra is Leslie-said-this or Leslie-thinks-that. Grrr.

2. Wen and Kim were spotted together riding their bicycles. (Azra heard this from Leslie, of course.) We tried to come up with words that express how much we loathe Kim but we couldn't think of anything strong enough.
3. Azra agrees that Calvin sounds great. She's super impressed that I tried to teach him to dance. I didn't tell her about the hand-on-butt incident (too soon, too painful), but I did ask if she thought the fact that he was nervous means he might actually like me. She wasn't sure. Then I got annoyed when she offered to ask Leslie. Since when did Leslie Dern become an expert?
4. Before she left, she gave me Smiley Quahog to cheer me up. She thinks I'm depressed. Ha!

Smiley Quahog stood on my desk, watching me as I wrote.

Everybody in our second-grade art class had made a Smiley Quahog. Mrs. Lachapelle had brought in quahog shells from the beach, and every kid got one and glued on a set of plastic eyes, a foam nose and cork feet. Azra had added yellow yarn for hair and a pipe-cleaner arm with a little plastic sword. He was a swashbuckling clam. Mine had disappeared years before, but Azra had kept hers, and she repaired it whenever parts fell off. For years we had been giving Smiley Quahog back and forth to each other as a joke gift.

I continued:

Why should Azra being Leslie Dern's lapdog bother me? It's not like Leslie is anything special. Being a junior counselor isn't a big deal either—it's got to be a boring job, right? I don't even want to be a JC anymore. In fact, now that I'm becoming new and extraordinary, I'm beginning to see Azra through clearer eyes. The girl is a follower. She lusts after Dean Eagler, just like everybody else. She likes Britney Spears, for God's sake. And now she's hanging out with Leslie Dern, the dullest person ever, instead of me. If the two of them were the only people in an otherwise empty room, they'd still have had a hard time standing out.

But for the New Floey, unremarkable just isn't good enough anymore.

Frank Sinatra glared at me disapprovingly when I climbed back on the bed.

"What are you looking at?"

He narrowed his eyes.

"What do *you* know?" I asked. "You're just a dumb ferret."

• • •

From the pages I'd printed off the Internet I read about Zen, about how it's more of an attitude or philosophy toward life than a religion. Zen says everything in the universe is connected in a kind of cosmic way, but we all get so focused on our own little worlds that we lose track of the big picture. Zen masters say that to really understand, we have to stop thinking so hard and just *feel*. They use little stories or riddles called koans to help open their minds. Koans don't always make sense, like "What is the color of the wind?" But meditating about them really hard is supposed to help people become enlightened.

Anyway, that's what I got out of it.

To me, the idea was kind of exciting. Didn't Azra say that thinking too hard was one of my problems? But recognizing a problem is the first step toward solving it, right?

The New Floey was already well on her way to enlightenment.

I concentrated on the color of the wind until my eyes felt heavy and I nodded off.

• • •

The sounds of loud running footsteps and shouting woke me. I'd been dreaming that Calvin and I were Zen masters in long yellow robes. We were dancing. In my dream these loud footsteps became the sounds of other dancers clomping around. They weren't very good dancers, or maybe they were just rude, because the music was soft and slow but their footsteps weren't.

I opened my eyes.

Another pair of eyes stared back at me. They were big and blue and very close to my own face.

I screamed.

"What are you doing?" my cousin Tish asked.

It took me a few seconds to recognize her. Finally, I said, "What are *you* doing?"

"Looking at your weasel. He looks old." Frank Sinatra was curled up on my stomach. He eyed my cousin suspiciously. "Aunt Grace said I could come in and say hello. We're going to be roommates."

I glared at her. Now that I *finally* had my own room it was so unfair that I, the New Floey Packer, had to share it with anyone, let alone a ten-year-old. This was definitely a setback.

Tish walked over to the other bed and bounced on the mattress. After a few bounces she said, "It'll do, I guess."

I sat up but didn't say anything.

She studied my black-and-white *French Kiss* and *Paris at Dawn* posters. "Those are nice. Have you had lots of boyfriends?"

I almost didn't answer. Finally I said, "No."

"Hmmm, that's too bad. Someday I'm going to have truckloads of them." She said that without even a hint of a smile. There was definitely something creepy about this pale, fat girl. She hopped up onto my bed. "This is nice. I wish I had a princess bed like yours."

I wasn't sure what a princess bed was, exactly, but I didn't like the sound of it. "It's not a princess bed."

She bounced again, and then out of the blue she threw herself backward with her arms spread out and her chubby legs dangling over the edge of the bed. She kicked her feet up and down. The sudden commotion did not please Frank Sinatra. He jumped off the bed and shot behind my chest of drawers.

"This is going to be great," she said. "I've never shared a bedroom with anyone, especially not somebody like you. Will you tell me what it's like to be a teenager?"

"I haven't been a teenager for all that long. I don't think I'm the best source of information."

"Probably not," she agreed. "I'd still like you to tell me what you can, though."

That's when I noticed Richard standing in the doorway, watching us. Seeing him again brought back the horrible memory of what I had learned the day before: this kid had seen the birthday picture.

"Hello, Floey," he said, smiling nervously at me.

"Hello, Richard," I said. "Tell me, where *is* that photograph?"

From his face I could see that he knew exactly what I meant.

Then Tish said, "What's *this*?" I turned to see what she was holding. It was my diary. I'd left it on my desk and now she looked like she was going to open it.

I leapt off the bed. "Don't touch that!"

"What is it?"

"None of your business."

She looked hurt but she put it down. "I wasn't going to rip it or anything."

"I bet I know what it is," Richard said. "I bet it's a diary."

"Well, I don't think it's any of your business what it is." I snatched it off the desk. I was obviously going to have to hide it somewhere.

"Then I must be right!" he said, raising his arms into the air triumphantly.

That's when I lost it. I put my face right up close to his and said, "Listen to me. This is my private life and you have invaded it. As long as you have to be here, we need to get a couple of things straight, Richard. First, you stay out of my room. And second, *you both better keep your grubby little hands off of my private things! Got it?*"

Richard blinked, his silly grin gone.

Then I heard my mother's voice. "Florence Abigail Packer! Is that any way for you to welcome your cousins?"

I turned and there she was in the doorway, looking even angrier than I was. "But, Ma—!"

She put her hand up to stop me. "There will be no more such talk in this house, young lady." And that was that. Once "young lady" comes out, there is nothing I can do. "I'm putting lunch together," she said, then turned and left us to go back to the kitchen.

As soon as she was gone, the obnoxious little boy smirked.

I wanted to pop him one, but I knew I'd never get away with it. Not here and now, anyway. If this was how it was going to be, I would have to deal with him later.

"Got it, creep?" I whispered, even closer to his face than before.

"Yeah," he said. "It's your private life and your private things. I got it."

Then I left the room as quickly as I could. I had to get out of there. I went out the back door and walked around to sit on the front steps. I opened my diary again.

Sunday, June 29, 1:10 p.m.

My Dear Self Yet to Come,

I hope you know how lucky you are! How I wish I were already you, because then the next three weeks would already be behind me! Twenty days to go and already I feel like a giant elephant just dropped a big turd on my head.

And then the phone rang.

"Floey, it's for you!"

In my emotional state, I forgot to ask who it was. That's why I was caught off guard when it turned out to be Wen. I'd been ignoring him for days.

"How are you doing, Floey?"

"Um, great," I said. "Just great."

I hated that I felt uncomfortable talking to him. He was supposed to be one of my two best friends in the world.

"Long time no hear from," he said. "You haven't been returning my calls. You okay?"

"Yeah, sure," I said. "I guess I'm just a little depressed."

"Really? Why?"

I thought about it for a moment. "Because I was dumped."

"You were? How can that be when you've never had a boyfriend?"

"I did," I said. "I was keeping it quiet. It doesn't matter now anyway. It turned out this guy didn't like me the way I liked him."

"You're kidding, Floey. Really? Who was he?"

I let him wait a few seconds. "I don't want to talk about it. It's too painful."

"Okay," he said. "I'm sorry to hear about that. I really am. I feel bad for you. Listen, I called because I wanted to say goodbye before I leave."

"Leave? Where are you going?"

"You forgot, didn't you? I have Wind Ensemble Retreat in Hartford. Remember? The van's picking me up in half an hour."

"Yeah? I guess I did forget. What's a Wind Ensemble Retreat?"

"Do you really want me to tell you, or are you just going to make fun of me?"

"I'm probably just going to make fun of you," I admitted, falling back into my normal comfortable self with him, but only for a moment. Wind Ensemble Retreat. Sounded like some artsy musical thing. Very Wen.

And then I had a moment of unhappy intuition. "Is . . . is Kim Swift going too?" Kim, I knew, played the flute.

"Yeah," he said. "She's going."

Figures.

Of course, I had Calvin now, sort of, but that didn't mean that the Wen-and-Kim catastrophe didn't still hurt. I thought of asking him what was going on between the two of them, but I couldn't bring myself to do it. I guess I realized that once I heard the news directly from him, my real unhappiness would begin. I didn't think I was ready for that. Not just yet. Besides, he wasn't offering the information, so who was I to push him?

"So," I said. "When are you coming back?"

"Thursday. Everybody needs to be back together by early Friday morning for the parade. You going to come watch?" Every year, the school band marches in Bristol for the Fourth of July.

"I guess so."

Then there was a long silence during which I wanted to hang up. But eventually he broke the quiet with small talk. Very forced.

"So, are you doing anything fun for the Fourth, after the parade?"

"Not really. We'll probably have a barbecue." Actually, we have a block party before the fireworks every year with our neighbors. It's a big deal on our street. But I didn't want to get into it right then.

"Yeah? Is Azra going?"

"Maybe."

He waited for me to invite him, but I didn't.

"Well, maybe I'll stop by too then. Would that be okay?"

Oh, great. Was he thinking of showing up with Kim? Wouldn't *that* be lovely.

"Fine."

Suddenly, I'd had enough of torturing myself. The New Floey took over.

"Okay, so out with it, Wendel. What's going on with you and Kim? Is she your girlfriend now or what?"

"Ahh . . . maybe," he said. Now I realized that the embarrassed note in his voice had nothing to do with the fact that I liked him. He was absolutely oblivious about that, I was sure. He had already admitted to Azra and me that he had never had a real girlfriend before. Kim would be his first. "I mean yes. I think she is."

"You *think* she is? What does that mean?"

"Well, we haven't officially said it yet."

"So have you kissed her?"

"Yes. Once."

"Then it's official," I said. "Good for you. Congratulations."

I was right—it *was* worse hearing it from him.

He ignored me. "Take care of yourself," he said. "And don't get too down in the dumps. Whoever he was, he sounds like a real jerk."

Our conversation ended quickly after that.

twisted broken flute
lying in the muddy grass
my pain knows no bounds

Sunday, June 29, 1:50 p.m.

Dear Experienced Me,

What is the matter with that woman? How can she call herself a mother? Okay, so Wen was never really my boyfriend. So what? She doesn't know that. In fact, I told her very clearly that he was. When is she going to even mention him? She seems to have no idea that I am deeply depressed. Doesn't she notice all the moping around I've been doing? When will I enjoy some motherly sympathy? It's been four whole days since Wen dumped me, and still she hasn't even asked about him!

The sad thing is, the longer she waits to ask, the guiltier she's going to feel when she finds out. Until she does, though, I'm certainly not going to tell her!

Okay, so I'm taking deep breaths and summoning a Zen calm. I need to meditate on ridding my system of Wen.

More deep breaths.

What would a real Zen master do?

I need to channel myself toward Calvin and the new me. I need to release my negative energy and concentrate on the important task at hand.

That afternoon, while my cousins were playing in our street with Billy Fishman and his friends, I scoured the newspaper. In the Happenings section I found what I was looking for: *The Devil's Coffeehouse. 826 Thayer Street, Providence. Monday, 7:30 p.m. Spoken Word Open-Mike Night.*

Sunday, June 29, 4:50 p.m.

beautiful calvin
where are you going tonight?
when will I find you?

chapterfive: in which i attend the devil's poetry reading

• • • • • • • • • • • •

"Floey," whispered Tish from the other bed. "Are you asleep?"

"Yes," I lied. "Fast asleep and having a dream. You woke me up."

"Sorry. I have a question for you."

I waited.

"What's it like when you have your period?"

I opened my eyes again. "Tish, what kind of a question is that?"

"It's a perfectly normal one. I'm just curious."

"Tish, that's a very personal question! Go to sleep."

We were quiet for a long time. Before she turned away she whispered, "I was just asking."

But I was pretending to be asleep.

Monday, June 30, 6:40 a.m.

Dear Floey of the (Hopefully) More Just and Peaceful Future,

Tish snores like some large animal fighting for its life. Like an angry walrus, maybe, or a dying caribou. It wouldn't be so bad if the rhythm were regular and predictable, but it's not. Every now and then she goes totally quiet for a really long time, and then just when I'm wondering if she's dead she suddenly gasps for air, so I practically jump out of bed. How am I supposed to get any rest through all that? It's like medieval torture! Worst of all, at the unholy hour of six in the morning, just when I finally fall asleep, she hops out of bed and stomps around the room until she finds my nice comfortable robe, and then she puts it on. Then she heads out to watch TV. So now I'm awake again! Honestly, it's unbearable!

Typical! I can't fall back asleep now. I keep trying to figure out how I can get to the Devil's Coffeehouse tonight. Ma would never ever let me go alone. She would never understand.

Oh, I just remembered the dream from my brief moment of sleep. Wen and Kim were in their band uniforms watching Richard hang copies of that terrible photograph all over town. They pointed and laughed. At the end of the dream Richard tried to suffocate me with a pillow, but I woke up and realized it was just Frank Sinatra sleeping on my face. (Note to self: IF THE PICTURE IS HERE, FIND IT ASAP!!)

When I came out of my room, my cousins were playing computer games. Robot blood dripped all over the screen. Good. This would give me a chance to clean their stuff without them watching and gloating.

It would also give me a chance to look through Richard's things.

I ran into the TV room (which had been transformed into a temporary bedroom for Richard) and closed the door behind me. Even though he'd been at our house for only one night, his room was a mess. He'd thrown his clothes all over the floor and his bed wasn't made. I rifled through his duffel bag. More clothes, computer magazines, but no birthday picture. I checked under the stuff he'd already dumped on the floor. Nope. I looked all around the room and didn't find the awful photograph anywhere.

Nothing.

That's when the door opened and Richard came in.

"What are you doing?" he asked.

At that moment I'd just gone back to rummaging through his luggage and was holding a fistful of his underwear. Now I calmly put the clothes back into the bag and zipped it back up, as if it were a perfectly normal thing for me to be doing.

"I'm cleaning up," I said.

He put his hands on his hips. "You're lying. You're looking through my stuff, aren't you?"

I kept a poker face and didn't answer.

"I'm right, aren't I? Yesterday you told us to stay out of *your* stuff, and here you are today going through *mine*. I'm going to go tell Aunt Grace."

"You never answered my question about the photograph," I said. I grabbed his arm. "Where is it?"

"Oh . . ." He pulled his arm away and turned around. He was in the doorway now, half in the room and half out. "So that's what this is about?"

I glared at him. "Is it here?"

He shrugged. "Maybe."

"What's that supposed to mean? Do you have it or not?"

He stepped back into the room and leaned thoughtfully against the door, closing it behind him. "Yes," he said. "I do."

"Then give it to me."

He shook his head. "I don't think so. You haven't been very nice to me. If you want it back so much, I think you should be nicer."

What nerve! *I* hadn't been nice to *him*? Who had locked me outside in the rain?

"Nicer to you or what? Or you'll put that picture up someplace where people can see it?"

As soon as I'd said it, I regretted it. His face changed as he thought about what was obviously a new idea I'd planted in his head. Slowly, he grinned at me.

"Maybe," he said. And then the supposed boy genius did the birthday-picture pose again, thrusting out his chest with his arms behind his head and his lips pursed. This time he also batted his eyes. He then left the room, swinging his hips as he went.

I stood frozen. What had I done?

Monday, June 30, 1:30 p.m.

To the Fabulous Floey of the Exciting Years Ahead,

Guess what? Wen just called. Can you believe it? And why did he call, you ask? Just to make sure I'm okay! He said he's worried that I'm depressed. He's clueless but sweet, don't you think? I told him I'm still on shaky ground. Anyway, he's in a college dormitory and it sounds like they're all having a great time. And the best news is that the girls (i.e., Kim) are staying in a different building altogether! (Big happy smile!!)

What is going through that ferret's head? I just caught him squirming in Richard's lap, clucking happily. This from the animal that nips at anything that moves. It's an absolute betrayal!

Big news: I have a plan for how to get to the poetry reading tonight—where I'll possibly see Calvin. Azra's coming with me. I'll meet her in front of the Y this afternoon to fill her in. Tonight is a WaterFire night in Providence so I'll tell Ma that we're going into the city to see the bonfires on the river with the JCs, and Azra will tell her parents she's going with my mother and me. If Ma makes a fuss because I'm not spending the evening with

Richard and Tish, I'll say I hardly saw my friends at all this week and I want to see them. It's not a lie. And if she says she wants to come along too and drag the little demons with her, I'll say it's a YMCA field trip and Azra had to get special permission just to bring me.

It's a perfect plan. Floey, you're a genius.

Okay, so maybe my plan wasn't *exactly* perfect. There was a snag, but only one: Ma would only let me go if I absolutely promised to spend the entire next day, morning, noon and night, with my cousins.

It was a big price to pay, but I made the promise.

Other than that, my plan worked. Azra and I took the bus into Providence after dinner.

• • •

The Devil's Coffeehouse turned out to be a long, dark room at the back of a bunch of stores. The only window was at one end of the room next to the entrance, so the deeper inside you went, the darker it got, even though it was still pretty light outside.

"Weird," Azra said.

I ordered coffee and she got a Coke. She stared at the walls, which were painted with all kinds of crazy graffiti and glow-in-the-dark scary faces. The Devil's Coffeehouse was a good name for this place. It looked like a dungeon or something. I could tell from Azra's expression that she didn't get any of this at all.

"Is he here?" she asked. When I'd met her at the Y, I'd sort of implied that there was a good chance we'd run into Calvin tonight.

I looked around. The place was almost full. Poetry readings must be more popular than I'd realized. Everyone sat at the dark tables sipping from mugs. Some of them talked quietly, but most of them stared up at the front corner of the room. The majority looked pretty normal, except for one table where everyone was dressed all in black with their hair dyed neon colors like orange or green. At the front end of the room there was a spotlight on a serious-looking girl in a tight T-shirt reading a poem about a dead bird. But no Calvin.

I shook my head.

"Are you sure you want to hang out with a guy who lurks around in a place like this?"

I ignored her. We took the only table left, which was against the wall, a couple of rows from the back. Even though smoking probably wasn't allowed, I could smell clove cigarettes. Azra started coughing. She has asthma. "Are you okay?" I asked her.

"I'm fine," she said, reaching for her Coke.

"You sure? Maybe we should go."

Still trying to control her coughing, she took a sip from her soda. "No, really. Let's stay a little while. He might show up." I watched her closely and a moment later she was better. She smiled. "I'm fine. I promise."

That's what I love about Azra. Even though this wasn't her kind of place, she put up with it because she knew it was important to me.

So we agreed to stay, for now.

I was a little disappointed that Calvin wasn't here, but mostly I was just nervous. Before we came I figured that as long as I was going to a poetry reading, I might as well read something. It would be an opportunity to be the new, visible Floey Packer. So I'd brought my haiku poems, including a new one:

out of the cold air
a tiny ray of sunlight
come in, meet my soul

All together, it wouldn't take long to read every poem I'd written. Still, I'd put my name on the reading list when I'd bought the coffee. Dead Bird Girl was reader number six. I was number eleven. It was a giant step for me. Old Floey would *never* have signed up to read poems in public, exposed like a fish in an aquarium. But even though she was fading, I could still feel her—my stomach felt woozy, my palms were sweaty and my heart was pounding pretty hard. I had to stop myself from gripping the table.

The girl finished her poem, everyone clapped, she sat down and somebody called out for the next reader. An old man with a big beer gut, number seven, stood up and ambled to the front of the room. I don't really remember his poem—I think it was about being afraid of flying or something like that.

I couldn't concentrate. I kept imagining myself in the light where the beer-gut man was standing.

waiting for my turn
a deer staring at headlights
fresh roadkill tonight

"You don't have to go up there," Azra whispered. "Look at you. You're a mess. Relax."

After the old man, the next one up was a young guy in a cowboy hat. I didn't really pay much attention to him, either. I hardly even looked at him. I had to force myself to stay in the chair and not run out the door. No matter how panicky I felt, I was determined to make myself go up there when they called my number.

Azra chewed on her straw.

I closed my eyes and tried to focus on the voice reading the poem. The cowboy spoke with long, slow vowels. His voice was strong and emotional and strangely familiar. In fact, the more I listened to it, the more familiar it sounded. I opened my eyes to get a better look at him.

I couldn't believe it.

"Oh my God, Azra," I said. "It's him."

"Him who?" she said. But then when she realized who I meant she practically sprained her neck trying to get a look.

"He's a cowboy? You didn't tell me he's a cowboy."

"Shhh!" I said. I was trying to watch and listen.

Out of his suit, Calvin looked different. He was still cute, but in an uncombed, scruffy, western kind of way. And his poem definitely wasn't haiku. I have to admit I didn't understand it, but it was full of loud dramatic parts and it seemed brilliant. It was long, and I remember he kept shaking his fist in the air and saying, *"Am I in your dream or are you in mine, Mrs. Fauntleroy?"* He said that a bunch of different times. The crowd seemed to love it because after the first few times they laughed and clapped whenever he repeated it. I didn't know who Mrs. Fauntleroy was, so it didn't mean anything to me.

Except in a Zen kind of way.

"Am I in your dream or are you in mine, Mrs. Fauntleroy?"

Even though I didn't know what it was supposed to be about, his poem really was good, much better than the one about the dead bird. I clapped and cheered along with everybody else.

Azra smiled too, but she was looking around like everyone was crazy.

Then I noticed that there was one other person who seemed particularly interested in what Calvin was saying. In fact, Calvin seemed to be reading directly to her. She was blond and pretty, and she was wearing a halter top and grinning proudly up at him.

Just like me.

Except for the blond and pretty part. And the halter top.

From the way she and Calvin looked at each other, it struck me that this was probably his girlfriend. That idea hit me like a sharp smack to my head. I hadn't thought of that possibility. Until now, it hadn't even occurred to me that he might have been interested in anyone but me.

"Am I in your dream or are you in mine, Mrs. Fauntleroy?"

I took a good look at her. Miss Halter Top really was pretty. Fifteen, maybe even sixteen. Perfect nose.

I hated her.

Calvin's poem got really dramatic now; his voice got louder and he waved his hand around even more than before. I watched him, my heart breaking.

That's when he paused in the middle of a sentence and I realized he was looking directly at me.

I wasn't the only one who noticed, either. It felt like everybody in the whole room turned to see what had stopped Calvin in his tracks. For a second or two, everyone stared at me.

And for one crazy, innocent, stupid moment, I was actually glad. I'm embarrassed to admit that for a split second the idea went through my mind that he might be happy to see me, that we'd talk after our readings and become good friends starting tonight. Eventually, I'd even be able to steal him away from Miss Halter Top. He'd fall madly in love with me—the kind of love you find in fairy tales.

But that fantasy ended when I recognized the horrified expression on his face. He suddenly turned white, with the same look, probably of shame, that he'd had after Lillian, Rebecca and Aunt Sarah had caught him on the sofa with me, hand on butt.

He tried to continue reading, but it wasn't the same as before. Somehow I'd thrown him completely off. He was quieter now, and he stammered through his own words. A couple of times he even lost his place. As he read the last few lines, he hardly moved his hands, and the final few times he said *"Am I in your dream or are you in mine, Mrs. Fauntleroy?"* it didn't have the same effect at all.

"My God," whispered Azra. "You must have made quite an impression on him."

When he was finally finished everybody clapped, but it was just out of politeness. A few people turned back to me again, probably to see if I was happy about ruining Calvin's poem. Calvin, on the other hand, didn't even look in my direction as he plopped himself down next to Miss Halter Top, who kept staring at me. What was going through her mind?

Number nine, an angry-looking woman with a crew cut, stepped up to the microphone.

"What do you want to do, Floey?" Azra asked me. "After this one, there's only one more and then you."

But I just stared at Calvin and Miss Halter Top. I was paralyzed.

The blond girl said something to Calvin and then looked back at me. They whispered a few things back and forth, but Calvin still wouldn't look at me. Finally, Miss Halter Top stood up and pushed her way through the tables toward me.

"Oh my God," Azra whispered behind her hand. "They're coming over here!"

A moment later, the girl was sitting at our table next to me. Behind her, Calvin looked really embarrassed.

Miss Halter Top looked me up and down. "So," she said, "are you the little girl who threw herself at Calvin the other night?" I didn't know what to say. She tilted her head. "Are you the little slut who tried so hard to steal my boyfriend? Was that you?"

Azra's eyes nearly bugged out of her head. I think she thought the girl might actually want to fight me. The idea had occurred to me, too.

"I . . . *no,*" I said. "I didn't exactly *throw* myself at him. Is that what he said?"

The girl glared at me. "Oh, I can read between the lines."

"Melanie, leave her alone," Calvin said. "She's only twelve."

"Thirteen," I corrected him.

She put her clenched fists on the table in front of her. "Why are you here tonight?"

Azra glanced nervously at me.

I stared back at this Melanie. "I was hoping to see Calvin again."

"I *knew* it!" she said over her shoulder to him. "Well, you saw him, little girl. Now I think you'd better leave."

Azra moved her chair back, but I shot her a look and she stayed put.

Calvin seemed really uncomfortable. "Come on, Mel . . . she didn't do anything wrong."

Melanie wasn't bigger than me—we were probably about the same size—but I wondered if she had a lot of experience fighting people.

"Well, I'm not going to leave," I said finally. "I'm going up to read. I wrote some poems."

Miss Halter Top stared at me for a long time. I wondered if she was going to throw the table over and lunge at me.

At the front of the room, the angry crew-cut woman was saying something about daffodils.

"All right, then *we're* leaving." The girl stood up. "Coming, Calvin?"

"Aw, don't be like that. . . ."

She didn't wait—she headed toward the door. He hesitated, but after a moment he followed her. At the exit he turned back to me one last time and mouthed a single word. *Sorry.*

And then he was gone. As simple as that. I never even got the chance to tell him I liked his poem.

Then a strange mixture of emotions ran through me. First, I felt a gush of relief that I hadn't been beaten up right in the middle of my first poetry reading. Next, I felt a brief moment of happiness because Miss Halter Top had actually been jealous. Soon after that feeling passed, though, all I felt was disappointment. How could Calvin let that girl treat him like that? And why hadn't he been happy to see me?

What was wrong with him?

What was wrong with *me*?

Azra stared like she was in awe of me. "Floey, are you okay?"

But I was thinking about fairy tales. You know the kind of happily-ever-after love you find in stories? Well, there's no such thing. It isn't real. It never really happens.

"Come on," I said to her. "Let's go home."

I heard somebody call out number eleven just as we stepped from the inside darkness of the café to the outside darkness of Thayer Street.

chapter six: karma or in which i am oblivious to the signs of sinister activity going on around me

• • • • • • • • • • • •

The next morning I read about karma, *dukkha* and impermanence. Zen teaches that karma is kind of like a reward system where you gain points when you do good deeds and lose them when you do anything bad. Dukkha, on the other hand, is chaos and suffering. It can strike anybody at any time, sometimes to make up for past bad karma and sometimes not. Impermanence is important too, because everything is always changing.

This is what I wrote in my diary:

Tuesday, July 1, 8:55 a.m.

Dear Florence,

I must either be suffering from bad karma or a heavy dose of dukkha. I can only hope it isn't permanent.

I know what you're thinking, Future Me. I'm a failure. I let myself down. I chickened out of doing the reading. I still have no boyfriend. Calvin turned out to be a loser and so did I. The New Floey will probably never exist. Instead, I'll probably always stay the same old me: ordinary, invisible and pathetic. Even worse, I have to keep my promise to spend the entire day with my evil cousins.

Ma's out playing doubles with Gary, so Richard told me to make him breakfast. Billy's with him too. I guess they're buddies now. Great. They demanded bacon and eggs. I wouldn't have made it for them except I was thinking about that photograph and, well, that's one problem I don't need right now.

I know. You don't have to say it.

I think I'll go flush my head down the toilet.

Lillian's postcards didn't exactly help my mood. We got two of them that first week. The first card said they were drinking piña coladas in front of the ocean in Cozumel, the first stop in their four-week trip through Mexico. The picture showed a beautiful white beach with grass huts, palm trees and pale blue water. I was jealous. The second card was addressed just to me. The picture was of a row of muscle guys standing together at some kind of outdoor bar. It was a wall of huge, triangular tanned backs and little muscular butts in tiny, brightly colored swimsuits. Lillian had only written a short message: "See anything you'd like to put your hand on?" At the bottom, she'd written: "My best to Calvin! (Oh, and Wen, too!)"

Ha ha.

Tuesday, July 1, 11:45 a.m.

Dear Future Me,

Who are you? Have you done anything important? Anything wonderful? Are you a great artist, a famous photographer, maybe a great writer? Did you find a cure for cancer? I want to know. It must be nice that everybody around you knows you're exceptionally gifted and amazing. You must be very happy.

Me? At this moment, I'm beginning to think Calvin was right: in the grand scheme of things some of us really are insignificant.

Especially me.

Richard and Billy spent a ridiculous amount of time playing at the computer. They'd sit there together for hours at a stretch. It was amazing how close they'd become in just a few days. Even when they dragged themselves away from the screen, Richard always seemed to hover around Billy. They played ball games on our street with some of Billy's neighborhood friends. Since Billy was twice Richard's size, they were like a planet and a moon, with Richard always somewhere in Billy's orbit.

Tish, on the other hand, didn't play much with the boys. She preferred to hover around *me*. That Tuesday morning, for example, when I tried sitting alone in the backyard reading a book (Richard and Billy had anchored themselves to the computer again), she followed me. The way I figured it, I'd promised my mother I'd stay with my cousins all day, but that didn't mean I couldn't ignore them.

Actually, Frank Sinatra was the first one to follow me outside. As I went for the back door, he planted himself right in my way. "I don't know why I should take you out," I said to him, "after the way you betrayed me." But he put on his cutest sad-eyed face. He's a manipulative ferret. Outside, wearing his harness, he sniffed around in the warm grass a few feet from my lawn chair. "That's right, traitor," I said to him. "You better keep your distance."

The ferret, of course, said nothing. But he didn't look sorry.

Moments later Tish came out and stood in front of me. My plan to escape my cousins had failed. "Why are you wearing that?" she asked.

I'd decided not to give up on the New Floey and felt like I needed a new look, so I'd gone into one of my sister's closets. She had a box of costumes from when she used to star in all the high school plays. I'd picked out a black fedora, like all the men wear in really old movies.

The New Interesting Floey Packer, I decided, wears an interesting hat.

"It's a statement," I said without looking up from my book, *Zen and the Art of Motorcycle Maintenance*.

She considered this and nodded.

I kept reading.

Tish settled herself into the chair next to me. "How

many times do you think about sex every day?" she asked. She was reading the questions from a personality quiz in a magazine. "Is it (A) almost never, (B) one to three times, (C) more than three times but not all the time or (D) constantly?"

I tried ignoring her but she wouldn't go away. She repeated the question.

"Can't you see I'm reading?" I finally blurted out.

"Which one? I'm testing your Sexual Enthusiasm Level."

"What? None of your business."

"All right, I'll tell you about me," she said. Along with the magazine, she'd also brought out a box of mini donuts. She popped one into her mouth. "I'm C. I think about it a lot."

"Okay," I said. "A. I never think about it."

"You're a liar," she said thoughtfully. "I'm putting you down for C." She ate another donut in one bite.

"How can you eat those?"

"Why shouldn't I? They're good."

"Don't you realize donuts are almost one hundred percent saturated fat? For a person so obsessed with boys, I'm surprised you eat like that."

"I don't care," she said with a shrug. "I'm a fabulous and talented person, and the fact that I'm overweight isn't going to stop boys from flocking to me like moths to a lightbulb." Then she smiled.

I glanced at the powder on her chubby fingers. If she continued this way, the girl could end up looking like a minivan. But she was so confident that I believed her—and still do even now.

Here I was trying to become fabulous at thirteen, while Tish was convinced she already was. And she was only ten.

"And I'm not *obsessed,*" she said. "Just preparing myself. Ready for question two?"

I looked back down at my book, but she didn't seem to notice my lack of interest in her test.

"Which of the following animals most closely represents your last boyfriend?" She looked up. "We could use our most recent crushes instead." Then she continued reading: "Is it (A) a pouncing tiger, (B) a cuddly teddy bear, (C) a scampering puppy or (D) a strutting peacock?"

I put my book down. "A scampering puppy? What kind of a boy is that supposed to mean?"

"Probably one who likes the girl to be in charge, like a mama's boy."

"What's *your* answer?"

She put her pencil to her pudgy chin and considered. "I guess A, a pouncing tiger."

"Really?"

"I think so. I don't know for sure, but I bet I'd like a boy who gets right to the point. What about you? Remember, it has to be about your last boyfriend or crush."

I almost said, "Too bad they don't have (E) an oblivious sea slug or (F) an insufferable weasel," but I didn't.

Frank Sinatra rolled his eyes as if he'd heard my thoughts.

• • •

As decreed by my mother, each morning during my cousins' stay I cleaned up their stuff. I did it as fast as possible, flying around the bedrooms picking up clothes and throwing them into the corners, shoving things under the beds and rushing the vacuum over the carpets. Usually, Richard's room was a disaster. He would just throw his dirty socks, pajamas and other stuff wherever he happened to be the moment he didn't need them anymore. But strangely, I thought, every now and then he made his bed—he wouldn't tidy anything else, just the bed. It was no big deal and it only happened every few days, but it was odd. Each time, I'd wonder if he'd realized I wasn't going to be his chef *and* his personal maid.

Tuesday, July 1, 12:40 p.m.

Wen called again. This time he just wanted to say hi and make sure I'm feeling better. We talked for almost forty-five minutes! He said they played music all day and his lips were starting to hurt. It was nice to talk to him, but kind of surprising, considering everything.

Hmmmm . . .

What's that you're asking, Floey of the Future? You want to know what's on my mind? Is it that obvious? I guess I can never get anything by you, can I? You notice everything.

Okay, so maybe you can help me understand something.

It's been two days in a row now, and Wen seems very very concerned about me. Is it my imagination, or does it seem, O my wise and enlightened future self, like these calls might be just a little bit more than mere friendly cheer-me-up conversations?

But that has to be just a crazy idea—me getting my hopes up, right? Why now? And what about Kim? Doesn't he still have her right there with him?

I wish you could come back and tell me what's going on here!

Still, no matter how you look at it, Wen is nicer than Calvin could ever be in his wildest dreams.

That afternoon, after I'd bicycled home from Gary's studio (even though Wen no longer worked there, I'd decided to keep going—I actually liked fiddling with all the equipment), Richard and Billy and their friends completely stopped what they were doing just to watch me. One minute they were playing in the street, shouting and laughing, and the next minute they were quiet. It's weird enough to have a crowd of people suddenly turn and stare at you, but when it's a bunch of little boys it's absolutely creepy.

I tried to ignore them and calmly got off my bike. Just as I was about to wheel it into its place under the stairs, Billy called out in that strange voice of his, "Are those things heavy to carry around?"

At first I didn't know what he meant, but when I looked at him and followed his gaze to my tank top I understood. He was staring at my chest. I crossed my arms to cover myself.

"Pervert!" I said.

The other little boys snickered.

On top of spying on me from his window, was Billy going to turn all the neighborhood boys into crude little jerks?

I shoved the bike under the stairs and stomped inside.

• • •

Wednesday night, Gary took Richard and Tish out to a Pawtucket Red Sox game. He even told my mother she didn't have to go. I think he just wanted to give her a break from taking care of my cousins.

"If your aunt Grace doesn't appreciate the beauty of baseball, there's no point in wasting the five bucks on a ticket," he said, winking at the kids. "We'll just go without her. Okey-doke?"

I had to hand it to him. He kept trying.

My mother gave him a little kiss on the cheek and his face went on red alert. It was sweet but sad.

Happily, nobody made a fuss when I said I didn't want to go.

So my mother rented *Love Me Tender*. My mother is a big Elvis Presley fan, so we sometimes rent his movies and watch them together. In this one, one of our favorites, Elvis marries his dead brother's fiancée, only to find that his brother, who was away fighting in the Civil War, isn't really dead—he comes back after the war expecting to marry his fiancée, who he still loves.

Another relationship shot to hell.

In the middle of the movie, I was thinking about how Gary kept doing nice things for my mother.

"Are you sure there's nothing going on between you and Gary?" I asked.

She reached for another handful of popcorn. "No, we're just friends."

"Positive?"

"Yes, I'm sure. Why do you ask?"

"I don't know. I think he likes you, and not just as a friend."

She shrugged but kept watching the TV. She didn't normally talk about stuff like this with me. My mother is a very private person. In that way she's the complete opposite of Lillian.

"Yes, I'm positive," she said eventually. And then she raised one eyebrow. "Is this a subtle message? Don't you see enough of Gary already? Do you want me to start writing him romantic notes?"

I studied her face. She was joking.

I had to laugh. I guess it really was a silly idea. My mother wasn't interested in dating anybody, and even if she had been, I couldn't imagine her with Gary. He was a nice guy and everything, but he just didn't seem like her type—too newspaper-and-slippers, too bald, too predictable.

Plus, it'd just be too weird.

"No," I said. "Actually, I think you're smart to stay uninvolved."

A little while later, out of nowhere she said, "I was thinking about Wen today."

"Yes?" I asked, keeping my voice steady. Finally, she was going to ask about Wen and me. Still, I didn't want to give anything away or make it too easy.

I waited.

But we were at one of the best parts of the movie, where Elvis is crazy with jealousy because he thinks his brother stole his wife away from him. By the time he'd hidden himself behind the big rock, waiting to shoot his brother, I knew she'd forgotten all about what she'd started to say.

I didn't remind her. If she wasn't going to ask me, then I wasn't going to tell her.

Wednesday, July 2, 10:30 p.m.

My Dear Friend and Confidant, Floey,

I just put the phone down. Since you're me, I don't have to tell you who called. Third day in a row. A whole hour this time. Anyway, you're not going to believe this (oh, what am I saying, of course you are!), but I worked up the nerve to ask him if he and Kim had finally made it "official." Remember what he said?

They broke up!! (Big giddy gasp!)

He asked me if it really counts as a breakup since

they only kissed once. (I said I wasn't sure.) But he says after the bus ride, when they got to the dorm, she told him she felt "uncomfortable"—and broke it off!!!

Ha! Woo-hoo!! (Shrieks of joy! Ecstatic cheers!!)

So what do you really think? Is it possible that he's been harboring a secret desire for me all this time? Maybe he only just realized it. In the history of relationships, it can't be so rare for best friends to become more than friends, right? Maybe Wen, unlike some people I could mention but won't (rhymes with Shmalvin), appreciates a good thing when he sees it—even if it did take him a while.

Am I on the right track or am I way off?

Could it be that he's ready to make his move, and that these telephone calls are his first timid steps?

You think so? Me too!

Oh my God. He'll be home tomorrow. I'll definitely see him either at night or at the parade on Friday at the latest. I wonder if it's going to be any different between us?

Terrible thought: What happens if it doesn't work out? After all, don't I know that getting my hopes up about this is a mistake? That it will probably only lead to heartbreak? I'd hate to lose Wen as a buddy.

And what about Azra? If only we hadn't agreed to share him—it makes everything so complicated!!

Oh well, I guess these are the kinds of problems you just have to deal with when you're dazzling, charming and hard to resist—bravo to Wen for finally noticing!

chapterseven: in which i sneak out of the house and finally have an adventure of my own or fireworks, stars and moons

• • • • • • • • • • • •

Thursday, July 3, 11:30 p.m.

Dear F,

Waited by the phone all day—almost lost patience with the boy, but finally he called! We talked for more than an hour!!

I practically have a boyfriend!!!

So, Wise Floey of Years Yet to Be, here's a question about early-relationship etiquette: Was it a bad idea for me to tell him that I missed him? Did I seem too needy? Should I have kept my mouth shut?

Was that completely dumb or do you think it was okay?

P.S.

I still feel guilty about Azra even though it's not my fault this is happening. After all, he is the one calling me every day, not the other way around.

Besides, HE SAID HE MISSES ME TOO!!!

How will I ever get through the long hours until tomorrow, when I'll finally see him? (Sigh!)

P.P.S.

Gary likes my hat. He said it makes me look exotic. Unlike my family (i.e., Ma, who keeps asking why I don't take it off inside the house), Gary has a refined sense of style.

I felt pretty confident as I got ready on Friday morning.

As the New Extraordinary Floey, I wanted to stand out at the parade, so along with my hat I wore dark sunglasses, and I tied a red silk scarf around my neck. I looked at myself in the mirror. The overall effect made a pretty strong impression.

Azra's mother wasn't a parade person but Azra was, so we picked her up at six-thirty in the morning. As soon as she got in the car she gave me that same puzzled look I'd seen at the poetry reading.

"What's with the costume?" she asked.

"It's not a costume. It's my new look. Do you like it?"

"It is? You look like a spy or something, maybe a blues singer."

"Or a blind gangster with a cold," suggested Tish.

Richard snickered. Ma didn't say anything—she just kept driving.

I ignored them all.

• • •

"There he is!" I shouted. "That's Wen!"

Azra and I screamed and called out, and my mother and Tish did too. I don't remember Richard joining in. He was probably off sulking somewhere. The band played some Dixieland song, not a regular marching tune. When Wen was about half a block away, he saw us and waved. Just then, the parade paused, so Azra and I ran over to him.

"Hey, soldier," Azra called out. "Love the hat!" Everyone in the band wore blue and white uniforms with shiny black shoes and tall blue helmets that made them look like toy soldiers. I could've just rolled the boy up in pita bread and eaten him.

"I'm so glad to see you," I said, realizing with disappointment that I'd left my hat and scarf by our blanket. I'd taken them off because of the heat. I tried to see if there was anything different about the way he looked at me, but it was hard to tell with all the confusion around us.

"How you doing, Floey?" he asked. "Finally cheered back up yet?"

I shrugged. "Not sure." I tried to send him a secret smile so he'd know I was thinking about him and me. "Maybe."

"Hi, I'm Floey's cousin Tish!" She was right on my heels. Sometimes having Tish around was kind of like having a dog.

"Hi, Tish," he said. "Nice to meet you."

"So," I asked him, "are we still on for this afternoon?"

"I think so. My dad made some plans, though. I might be late."

I was disappointed, but only a little. As it turned out, Azra had said she wasn't coming to our block party after all because her mother decided at the last minute to throw a barbecue with their own neighbors. Azra had invited my mother, my cousins and me to her house after the parade but fortunately Ma said no. This meant, I'd realized with secret excitement, that if Wen came I was going to have him all to myself.

"Well," I said. "Guess I'll see you later, then."

And that was all the time we had, because the band started playing again and Wen had to step back in line. He and the rest of the band did a hilarious dance where they marched in place and then side to side and then turned around and did it again. The crowd went wild. So did we.

After they marched away, Tish asked, "That's the boy from the picture, isn't he? Are you *sure* he's not your boyfriend?"

"Who, Wen? No." I glanced at Azra, but I don't think she was listening. "We're just friends, that's all. I already told you I don't have a boyfriend."

"Oh," Tish said. "He's *soooo* cute! He's *adorable!*"

We walked back to our blanket.

I couldn't even look at Azra.

Friday, July 4, 11:00 p.m.

Dear Florence,

Wen didn't show up.

I spent the whole barbecue waiting on our top steps so I could listen for the phone. I left a couple of messages on his machine but he never even called back. While I waited, every front yard on my street was full of people. Everyone had fun except me.

Wen better have a good excuse. I hope for his sake that he was kidnapped by aliens.

Richard's little friends made the day even worse. First, they kept peering over at me from Billy's yard. It's really starting to bug me. In a world where hardly anybody notices me, why do these little boys find me so fascinating? Then later, Richard and Billy nearly blew me up with a firecracker. They threw it up on the step, but I heard the hissing and brushed it over the side just in time. I went ballistic. But when I demanded that Ma and Mrs. Fishman make them stay inside for the rest of the day, they refused. Typical! There is no justice!

After that, Tish sat with me for a while and I had to listen to her go on about how she's going to be a writer someday. Apparently, she writes adventure stories about people with magical powers, like wizards and witches. She also kept saying how cute Wen is and how it's obvious that I think so too. (Where's the nearest bridge? I want to jump off!)

When everyone went to the beach to watch the fireworks, I stayed home like an idiot to wait for Wen's call. I told Ma I wasn't feeling well. It wasn't exactly a lie.

So now I'm here in bed, wide awake in the dark, writing to you using my penlight. How did I let myself get so carried away again? Am I destined to grow old alone, invisible and forgotten, forever searching for something that doesn't exist? Will I die on some cold floor, my decomposing body lying for days unnoticed and unloved, waiting by a phone that will never ring?

Why is everything going wrong? Even this diary seems to be plotting against me. Here I am in the middle of a crisis and it runs out of pages. How can I express myself with only one line left?

Stupid diary. Stupid day. Stupid me.

I stared up at the darkness, silently considering my own stupidity.

Pathetic! Weak! Dumb, dumb, dumb! What happened to independent? What happened to self-sufficient? What's wrong with me?

That's when I heard, or at least I *thought* I heard, a tapping sound from my window. *Ploink*. A moment later, it happened again. *Ploink. Ploink.* It was the sound of something small hitting the screen.

Then somebody outside whispered, "Floey!"

I sat up and lifted the shade. There were two flashlights in the darkness just under my window. It was Wen and Azra.

"What are you doing?" I called, ecstatic to see them but trying to be as quiet as I could.

"Getting you out of bed!" whispered Azra, nearly blinding me with her flashlight.

"Are you crazy?"

"Sorry I couldn't come earlier. George and I had to take care of two needy parents." George was Wen's little brother. Wen set his backpack on the ground. "But it's not that late. Want to go to the secret beach?"

The secret beach was a little sandy clearing that Azra, Wen and I had found behind a patch of reeds along Otis Cove. As far as we knew, nobody else knew about it. It was our special place where we liked to go together.

I turned around to see if the lights and voices had woken Tish, but she looked comatose. Actually, without even looking I should have known she was asleep because it sounded like there was a wild growling beast in the room.

"Sure, if you insist," I said, trying to sound casual so they wouldn't know how happy I was. "Just give me a second to change."

I glanced again at Tish but she definitely looked dead to the world.

Sneaking out of the house in the middle of the night was the sort of thing Lillian used to do, not at all an Old Floey thing. Thrilled, I threw on some clothes, including my hat and scarf, as quietly as I could. I carefully lifted the screen, hooked one leg over the window and pushed myself through. Then I hopped down to my friends.

My escape successful, I was ready for whatever adventure the night might bring. And oddly enough, that night something really really weird, something strange and adventurous, actually did happen.

"My God, Floey," Wen said. "What are you wearing?"

"Let me introduce myself," I said. "You're looking at the New Improved Floey Packer."

• • •

Otis Cove was just off the main road that led into the center of Opequonsett, not too far from Wen's house. There was a secluded area of sand in the middle of a thick patch of reeds by the water that probably belonged to an old vacation cottage. There wasn't much light from the sky that night, so I was glad I'd thought to bring my little penlight. We'd been here many times but never at night.

After we sat down in the sand, Wen opened his backpack and took out a medium-sized box. "For you and me," he said, opening it up. It was a cake, the kind you buy in the junk-food section of a grocery store.

I stared at it. "Why?"

Squinting into the beam from my penlight, he held his hand up to block his eyes. "For surviving our first breakups."

Oh, he was so *sweet*!

"I didn't know you get a cake for that."

"Apparently," he said, slicing a piece for each of us, "you do."

"So this is Dump Cake?"

He laughed.

Azra didn't. She knew I had told Wen that I'd been dumped by some mysterious guy. When she'd asked me why, I'd told her the truth: that when he asked me why I sounded depressed I had a moment of insanity. She'd just said I was weird. She wouldn't give me away, though.

Wen nodded sympathetically. "I know you've been through a hard time."

Azra rolled her eyes.

"It's nothing," I said carefully. "It's not a big deal."

"So who was he? How come I didn't know anything about him?"

I couldn't tell the truth, that it was *him,* so I had to make something up. "I was embarrassed," I began. "He was . . . just a pen pal. We wrote each other letters, but the truth is I hardly ever saw him." I felt guilty for lying again, but secretly I also felt proud of myself. It was a pretty good story.

"Oh really?" Azra said, giving me a you're-crazy look. "Tell us more."

What was she doing? "Well . . . I met him at summer camp when I was little. We sent each other notes for years. It's just stupid. That's why I never said anything."

But Azra didn't leave it at that. She was having fun with me. "What was his name?"

I flashed her a warning with my eyes. I felt bad enough already, and she was making it worse. "Robert," I said. It's the name of the guy who wrote *Zen and the Art of Motorcycle Maintenance*. "But I really don't want to talk about it anymore. Can we change the subject?"

"Sure," Wen said. "I completely understand." He handed me a slice of cake on a paper plate.

"Thank you," I said, relieved. I studied his eyes for signs of secret passion. Unfortunately, it was too dark to be sure.

The Dump Cake was good. It was dry with hard frosting that tasted kind of plastic, but that didn't matter. It was absolutely delicious.

"It's great to be here," Wen said, kicking back in the sand. "Just us. The Three Blind Mice." I wondered if he was trying not to act suspicious in front of Azra. He seemed to be working hard on keeping our little secret, so I decided to follow his lead. We would have to find time to discuss our secrets another day.

A warm breeze blew my hair into my face. Azra told us about being a day-camp junior counselor and Wen talked about his retreat. We grilled him about Kim. He said he'd been sad at first, but now he was practically over it. Then I told them about how hard it had been at home with my monster cousins. Azra and I even told Wen about Aunt Sarah and the birthday picture. It felt good to talk with them about it. Wen laughed about the picture, and so did I, a little, so I guess Azra felt okay to laugh too. When I saw it from someone else's point of view, it really was kind of funny.

I sliced myself another piece of Dump Cake. We sat quietly for a while and watched as somebody on the other side of the Narragansett Bay lit the last fireworks of the day. Bright colors burst across the sky. Reds, blues, greens, one after another. It was fantastic, like our own private show. It occurred to me that this could have been incredibly romantic, if only Azra hadn't been there. But then I felt bad for thinking that way. Azra and Wen and I were best friends.

"I have a question for both of you," Azra said, startling me out of my thoughts. "Leslie Dern's sister told her that Dean Eagler's parents are going away with his little brother later this month, and Dean's having a big party. Leslie and the JCs want to crash it. You guys want to come?"

Leslie again. Grrr.

"Another party?" Wen asked as sparkling pink fire shot up from the horizon and fell back down without bursting. "How does he get away with it?"

"I don't know. Oblivious parents. But it'll be great."

"A high school party?" he said. "Maybe I'll come. I don't know."

So then Azra waited for my answer.

"I don't think so. Why should we go to a party full of girls slobbering over Dean Eagler?" I looked directly at her. "Doesn't that just seem a little pitiful?"

"For your information," she said slowly, the flashlight making long dark shadows on her face, "I do not slobber over Dean Eagler. You must be thinking of somebody else."

As a matter of fact, Azra had often told me how beautiful she thought he was. I even remembered her considering out loud what she might give if only she could be locked in a closet with him for fifteen minutes.

But I didn't say so. There wasn't any point.

"Sorry, I didn't mean anything by that. It's just that I don't want to be so predictable and ordinary." And then, thinking of her at the party standing in the middle of a pack of giggling girls swooning over Dean, I said, "Neither should you."

She tilted her head. "What makes you so superior all of a sudden?"

Fortunately, Wen spoke up before it got even worse.

"I'll go, but only if Floey goes too. It'll show that she's really over being dumped."

It took me a moment to realize the significance of this, but when I did it pulled me back into the present. Aha! Here was absolute proof that Wen was interested in me! Clever boy!

I tried to think of something equally clever, some response that would seem just as innocent but would actually be full of secret meaning. But I didn't get a chance. Because somebody laughed.

Somebody who wasn't Wen or Azra or me.

That's when the really really weird thing started to happen.

Wen sat up. "What was that?"

Now, we had been to our secret beach many times before, but never so late. Still, even during the day we'd never seen anyone else using it. Who would come here at such a strange time? It was midnight! In a moment of pure terror, I imagined some horrible lunatic with a chainsaw. The person laughed again, and then there was another voice, whispering, getting closer. We sat as still as we could. The voices were coming from the reeds to our left. It occurred to me that they might be the people who really owned the cottage. Whoever they were, they were making their way through the reeds toward us.

"Quick!" I whispered. "Flashlights!"

With our lights out, it was almost completely dark around us. On the other side of the little clearing, another light moved through the reeds, getting closer. Our visitors had their own flashlight. Suddenly, the wall of reeds opened up and somebody stepped into the sandy area.

"Such a beautiful night," whispered a man's voice, a pretty large man, as far as I could tell from the shadow. In fact, he looked as big as a bear.

"Glorious!" a woman said. She'd stepped out of the reeds a moment after the man did. "Even prettier than last night."

We were at the edge of the clearing. If these people had only known where to point their flashlight, they could have easily caught us sitting there, so we stayed absolutely quiet and still.

The man turned his light back to the reeds and two more people climbed through to our little sandy area. Even though I couldn't see the man with the flashlight, I got a brief look at the other three. When I saw them, I stopped breathing. I was close enough to Wen to feel him almost jump too.

These people weren't wearing any clothes.

They were completely, absolutely stark naked.

There was an old bald man, big and powerful-looking, with a huge belly and a blurry tattoo on the back of his arm. He was holding hands with a skinny old woman with long white hair to her waist. As they stepped into the clearing, they were laughing about something. The person standing next to the man with the flashlight was another old woman, this one with short curly hair and big droopy breasts, but I only saw her for a split second. They all looked really old, maybe in their seventies. Whenever the light passed over any of them, Azra, Wen and I could see everything there was to see.

Everything.

Without intending to, we suddenly knew an awful lot about these strangers, the most private things.

I was horrified.

Under his breath, Wen said, *"Holy—!"*

I elbowed him. He'd said that almost loud enough to be heard. Thankfully, the naked people were still laughing and didn't seem to notice.

I felt incredibly guilty. These people probably *were* staying in the old cottage, so they had a right to be here, unlike us. Every now and then the light gave an unpleasantly clear view of something I'd rather not have seen: secret hair, saggy skin—I didn't want to know about any of it. Even though it wasn't on purpose, it was terrible that we had invaded their privacy, and in such an awful way. But what could we do?

I was too scared to move.

The two old couples, still holding hands and giggling, ran down the beach and into the water. In the moonlight I watched the large man and the woman with the droopy breasts sit down in the shallow water and splash each other. The second couple ran in deeper. I remember looking at the bald guy and thinking that for a man with such a huge stomach, he had a surprisingly dainty butt.

After that thought, I felt even worse.

Then it suddenly occurred to me that these old couples were in love. Okay, so they weren't beautiful or special as far as I knew, but they certainly looked at each other like there was magic going on. Maybe that sounds stupid, but that's what I saw. They might have been old, but it sure looked like they still had romance in their lives.

Wen tugged my arm and all three of us dashed into the reeds behind us. I only just managed to keep hold of my penlight. We were quick, but we made a lot of noise.

They must have heard us because one of the men called out, "Who's there?" And then, "Did you hear that?"

We ran away through the reeds as fast as we could. Maybe they would mistake us for a raccoon or something. As I ran, I found myself comparing those old couples to Calvin and me and every other unsuccessful relationship I knew about. Why was it different for these people? What was their secret? How did they find that kind of real and lasting happiness? Later, that question, the Mystery of the Old Naked People, would run through my mind over and over again.

We hopped on our bikes and pedaled as fast as we could. Only when we reached the cemetery, a safe distance from the cove, did we slow down enough to talk.

"Did you see that?" whispered Wen. "Can you believe it?"

Azra looked traumatized. "That was absolutely disgusting. So gross."

I didn't say so, but I couldn't help thinking she had missed the point.

"Don't ever mention this to anybody," Wen said. "I don't ever want them to find us out."

"Maybe they're still coming after us," Azra said.

"You think?" I asked.

"I don't know, but I'm going home."

The streets flew under my wheels and the houses raced by one after another. And my heart kept pounding. I felt a strange excitement because I had finally had an actual adventure of my own. At last, my good karma must have been paying off. I couldn't wait for Lillian to come back from her honeymoon so I could tell her.

chaptereight: three guys or zen and the art of flirting

• • • • • • • • • • • •

I climbed back through the open window to my bedroom as carefully as I could so I wouldn't make any noise. Unfortunately, as I stepped through the window my shoe caught on the trellis, so I lost my balance and fell onto my bed, accidentally squashing Frank Sinatra. His squeal could have woken the dead. It was loud enough, at least, to wake Tish, and that was saying something. The ferret scrambled away as soon as I hopped off him, but by that time it was too late. The shadow in the other bed sat up.

"What are you doing?" she asked me. "Where did you go?"

"None of your business." I scrambled down from the bed and yanked off my hat, scarf, shoes and pants. I was worried that my mom might come to the room to find out what had made such a racket. Oh God! Why did I have such terrible luck?

Tish adjusted her pillow so she could sit back against the wall. "This is great! Did you know that my mom told

Richard and me to watch out for you? She said you might be a bad influence. Did you know that?"

"She said *what*?"

"I was hoping she was right, and now I think she was. I'm so glad! Where did you go? Did you meet a boy somewhere?"

What nerve!

"I already told you it's none of your business."

"Then I must be right. Was it Wen?"

"All I know," I said, hopping into bed, "is that you better not say anything about this to anybody." I put my head on my pillow, and for a while neither of us spoke. I could even hear the crickets outside.

"Here's the deal," Tish whispered after a few minutes. "You tell me where you went tonight and who you were with, and I won't say anything to Aunt Grace."

I sat up and stared at the shadow in the opposite bed. "You wouldn't dare."

"Sure I would. Tell me."

She waited quietly while I considered the situation. "Okay," I said eventually. "Suppose I do. How do I know you won't blab everything anyway?"

"You can trust me. And while we're at it, I have lots of other questions too. Personal questions. You're going to have to tell me what I want to know. Not just tonight, but anytime I want."

"Personal questions? What kind of personal questions?"

"I don't know, lots of things. I want to know what it's like to be a teenager. What's it like to be pretty and popular? I keep asking you about things but you don't answer me."

Pretty and popular? That was a laugh!

I had to think fast. I was probably off the hook with my mother for the moment, because if she hadn't come to investigate the noise by then, she probably wasn't coming at all. But after years of witnessing just how mad she got whenever she caught my sister after one of her adventures, I knew things would get ugly for me if Tish told her about tonight. At the same time, though, I didn't want to let a ten-year-old walk all over me.

"All right," I said. "But not any old time you want, just tonight. And just one question."

The dark lump shook her head. "No. You have to answer every question I have or I'll tell."

"No deal, Tish," I said, trying to sound confident. "You get this one question for sure and that's all I'll guarantee. If you ask me another, I might answer and I might not. If you don't like that deal, go tell, but then you definitely won't get anything out of me. And I mean *ever*."

We both sat quietly for a long time and I wondered if I'd pushed my luck too far.

"Okay," she said finally. "*Two* questions tonight and it's a deal."

Relieved, I lifted my head again. "All right. Where was I? On the beach at Otis Cove. That's one question. Who was I with? I was with Wen, you were right. Whoop-dee-doo. But Azra was there too. That's two. Now I have a question for *you:* Does Richard really have the birthday picture?"

"Birthday picture?"

"You know exactly what I mean. Does he?"

There was a long silence before she answered. "I really don't know what you're talking about."

I dropped down to the pillow. I didn't believe her—I figured she must know. But what could I do?

"So Wen really is your boyfriend, isn't he?"

I pulled the covers up to my neck. "That's your third question. I'm not going to answer any more. Now, while you think about how long you're going to keep asking me that over and over again even though I won't answer it, I'm going to sleep." I closed my eyes. My heart raced. What did I do to deserve twenty nights with this nosy little girl?

Eventually, Tish slid down into her bed again and put the pillow back under her head.

"Good night, Floey," she whispered.

Just then, another series of explosions went off outside. I imagined big globes of fire and color somewhere overhead.

Saturday, July 5, noon

Dear Me,

Do ferrets ever lose so much hair they go bald? I've heard of hairless cats. Ma found a huge hairball under the kitchen table and told me to clean it up, as if it were my fault. She made me redo all the carpets! I got back at her, though, by singing "We Shall Overcome" in a loud voice the whole time. Ma pretended she didn't hear me, but I know she did.

Once again, New Floey does what Old Floey never would have dared! My voice is a little hoarse now, but it was worth it. In fact, it actually sounds sort of sexy. Kind of Demi Moore-esque. Maybe I should call Wen so he can hear me.

On second thought, I'll wait. He should call me.

Yuck! Richard is such a pig! Just now, Ma leaves the house for only a minute, and as soon as the door closes behind her what does he do? He runs into my room, drops his pants and farts right near my face! Gag! Barf! Billy was at the door, laughing. Truly, they are barnyard animals!! Plus, the boy is sickeningly sweet to Ma but she doesn't seem to have the faintest clue that it's all an act. I tried to tell her but she just said I have a bad attitude. His room this morning was an absolute pigsty as usual—except he'd made his bed again. I bet he does that to get in good with Ma.

Fourteen long days to go until my cousins leave and I'm free.

My good karma must be sky-high by now!

P.S.

I need to get myself another hardcover diary soon. Writing in this spiral notebook just isn't the same. It feels like I'm doing homework.

That afternoon I ran into Calvin in the bookstore café next to Gary's studio. By then it was raining, so I was waiting for Ma to pick me up. If I had noticed him sitting engrossed in a book at the next table I wouldn't have sat down. In fact, if I'd known he was there I would have stayed hidden in the studio with Gary. But I didn't recognize him until it was too late. He saw me. We were too close to pretend we didn't know each other.

"Hello, Floey," he said, almost knocking over his tea.

Talk about dukkha. I almost died of embarrassment right there over my decaf caffe latte.

"Uh, hi, Calvin," I managed, my face growing hot. "How are you?"

He fidgeted a little and gripped his cup nervously with both hands. At least he had the courtesy to be uncomfortable. He looked different in a T-shirt than he did in either his suit or his cowboy hat. Skinnier. Plus, I noticed a big pimple at the corner of his mouth.

After a moment of awkward silence he said in his slow Oklahoma way, "I . . . I'm sorry I couldn't stay that night to hear you read your poems."

"Oh, that's all right." For some reason, I didn't want to tell him that I hadn't gone through with it. "They weren't anything, just some haikus."

He stared at me. "You write *haikus*?"

"Well, like I said, they weren't anything. Besides, you had to go."

He looked even more uncomfortable, but he nodded. "Yeah, sorry about all that."

There was another long silence. And then I don't know what came over me—I opened my mouth and the words just popped out before I could stop them. "Do you always let that girl push you around?"

His shoulders rose a little. "Oh, Melanie's nicer than you probably think," he said. "She was just having a rough day is all. She's a little high-strung, but she's all right. If you knew her, you might even like her."

I had a hard time imagining it. All I could think of was how he'd let her bully him out the door.

small frightened mousie
whatever happened to my
zen cowboy poet?

I checked out the window for Ma's car but didn't see it. Today, of all days, I hoped she wouldn't be late.

"Are you waiting for somebody?"

"Yes, my mother. She's picking me up." And then I felt like I had to explain further, so I said, "I work part-time at the picture place next door. I'm kind of a photographer."

"Really?" He glanced at my fedora, black blouse and black skirt. I'd chosen a goth look today. "In that outfit you certainly *look* like an artist."

I studied his face to see if he was making fun of me, but I decided he wasn't. "Listen," I said. "I didn't get a chance to tell you that I really liked your poem."

"You did?"

I nodded. "I don't think I understood it completely, but I liked it—in a Zen kind of way."

He looked surprised. And then, out of the blue, a big,

shy grin formed on his face. "Thanks," he said, suddenly staring down at his cup. For a couple of seconds, he didn't look at me. I could tell I'd really made him happy. It was actually kind of sweet. "Believe it or not, that's exactly what I meant it to be—a Zen kind of poem. You're the only one who noticed."

"Well, I did. And I honestly liked it a lot."

A moment later, he leaned over to see the cover of my book. "Wow," he said. "*Zen and the Art of Motorcycle Maintenance*. Do you know that that's one of my favorites?"

So we talked about it a little, and that led me to ask him about what *he* was reading. It was a worn copy of *The Collected Poems of T. S. Eliot*. Calvin said he couldn't count how many times he'd read it. After that, we both relaxed a little and started talking about books. It turned out that he's an even more avid reader than I am, and not just of poetry. Pretty soon, we were telling each other all about ourselves. He told me how his family moved up from Oklahoma just before he started eighth grade. It had been hard for him to adjust at first because he didn't know anybody, so he'd spent a lot of time reading. That's when he had discovered poetry.

"Is Melanie a poet, too?"

"Melanie?" He smiled and shook his head. "She comes to see me at open-mike nights every now and then, but she says she doesn't really get it. It isn't her thing."

As we spoke, I realized that talking to him had suddenly become comfortable and easy again, like it had been at the wedding. Only this time, I told myself, I wasn't interested in him as anything other than a friend. And that made it almost nicer.

That's when I noticed Ma's car finally pulling into the parking lot.

"I have to go," I said.

"Sure," he said, setting his empty teacup down in its saucer. "I do too, pretty soon."

I stood up and grabbed my things. I don't know why, but before I left I said, "I'm sorry about what happened. At the wedding, I mean. It was really embarrassing."

His face went pink. "It's okay. It wasn't that big a deal, really. I enjoyed dancing with you. You're a good dancer."

"I know you told Melanie about it, but don't tell anybody else, okay?"

"I won't."

I smiled. "Well, bye, then. Nice to see you."

"Bye." But before I got as far as the door he said, "Hey, Floey. I'm really glad we ran into each other again."

I waved and left him sitting by the window.

On the way home, I went over our conversation in my mind. What a shame it was that he liked Miss Halter Top. He seemed like he might be a nice guy. Sweet, even. But then I remembered what he'd all but said at the wedding—that I'm too young for him. He was starting tenth grade in the fall, so even if he didn't already have a girlfriend, he probably wouldn't want to be seen with a soon-to-be eighth grader like me.

But that was okay, I decided as we rode through the rain.

I already had Wen. Plus, I didn't like Calvin in that way anymore. I was over him.

I was *so* over him.

Sunday, July 6, 8:00 p.m.

After spending the entire day in Mystic with my cousins I had every right to expect a message from a certain trumpet player when we got back—after all, it's been two days! But what did I find? Nothing! Nada! What is the matter with that boy? I'm getting seriously tired of waiting for him again and again. What kind of pathetic boyfriend does he think he is? This is it! I'm giving Bugle Boy until tomorrow morning. After that, he can go eat another Dump Cake.

The next day I biked to the drugstore to buy tampons and a new diary. Standing in line to pay, I noticed that the clerk behind the counter was Dean Eagler.

Is it humanly possible to stop yourself from blushing by sheer force of will? Why do some people go red in the face all the time while others get to experience their embarrassment in private? Can anybody tell me?

I would have put the tampons back but he saw me before I got the chance.

"Can I help you?" he said.

Dean Eagler, the secret fantasy of almost every girl I knew, looked kind of like Elvis, with the same dark, brooding eyes, slicked-back hair and sexy lips. Behind the counter he was the moody Elvis, like the one in *King Creole*. Very cool. It didn't matter that he didn't know or care that I existed—there was still no way I was going to buy tampons from him. Without dropping my eyes, I casually let go of the package so it fell on the floor. Since the counter was between us, he couldn't see anything below my waist. To cover the sound, I coughed just as the box hit the ground.

"Excuse me," I said, hacking. "I think I'm catching a cold."

He took my new diary and waved it over the scanner. As he waited for the receipt, I caught him sneaking a glance at me. All of a sudden and completely unexpectedly, he smiled.

"Wait a minute—you're Floey Packer, aren't you?"

"Uh, yes . . ."

His smile got even wider.

Keep in mind that a smile from Dean Eagler, one of the best-looking guys on the planet, was no small thing. His was a mysterious, rock-star kind of smile, and I have to admit it made my knees wobbly.

"I'm Dean Eagler," he said, holding out his hand. I didn't know why he was holding it out, but I shook it. "I like your hat," he said.

Inside, I did a victory dance.

"Well," he said, "it sure is nice to meet you in person."

I wasn't sure what he meant by "in person," but at the time I was busy wondering why he was talking to me at all.

The New Floey was already attracting attention.

"Listen," he said, flashing me yet another of his moody Elvis smiles. "I'm having a little shindig. Week after next. You gonna be around?"

Wait. Hold on. Did he just invite me to his party?

Was he actually *flirting* with me?

"I don't know. Maybe. Yes."

He put my new diary in a plastic bag and handed it back to me. "Great. Sunday, the twentieth. Around eight. My folks don't clear out until that afternoon. You know where I live?"

I nodded.

He leaned on the counter and his voice dropped a little. "One other thing—it's kind of hush-hush."

I nodded again, and he winked at me. I was just about to rise off the ground and float away when a high voice interrupted. "Excuse me," it said. I turned and there was Billy Fishman. "I think you dropped something."

And then *It* appeared on the counter between us, big and blue and obvious.

I nearly screamed.

The box practically shouted out, *"ATTENTION! THIS WOMAN IS HAVING HER PERIOD!"* But Billy's expression was a perfect picture of innocence. I had to think fast. I only had a second or two before my face would turn beet red again. Denial, I decided, was the cleanest way out.

"Not mine," I said. I turned away and left as quickly as I could.

Monday, July 7, 6:30 p.m.

Dear Fab Floey,

I have an invitation to Graceland sent directly from the King himself! Who needs a trumpet player when I have Elvis?

And he likes my hat!

Wen is so part of the past. Get this: He finally called this afternoon, but only to tell me that today is Ringo Starr's birthday. He was a Beatle, apparently. Ringo Starr. I mean, honestly!

I informed Ma that we're watching Blue Hawaii tonight. If Richard and Tish don't like it, they can go and sulk.

chapternine: dukkha

There's a Zen story about a man hiking through the jungle who accidentally walks right up to a vicious tiger. He turns and runs as fast as he can and eventually finds himself at the edge of a cliff. Since the tiger is right behind him, he has to climb down a vine and dangle in the air over a drop that would definitely kill him if he fell. As he hangs there, a mouse starts gnawing at the top of the vine. Suddenly, the man notices a wild strawberry growing on the vine. He eats it. It's the most delicious strawberry he's ever tasted.

I was thinking of this story while making a crosshatch pattern in the peanut butter I was spreading to make Richard's sandwich. It was midday on Tuesday, and Ma had told me to make lunch for my cousins while she went out for a minute. Frank Sinatra was licking himself in a disgusting way right in the middle of the kitchen floor.

On top of the crosshatches, I made a happy face.

Like the man on the vine, even in the middle of hardship I was finding something to enjoy.

Then the phone rang.

I nearly tripped over Frank Sinatra, but it hardly fazed him at all. I grabbed the phone. It was Azra.

"I can't believe you!" she said. "You've been holding out on me! Why didn't you tell me *everything*?"

"What didn't I tell you?"

"About Lillian's wedding—about what happened! You left out the most important part!"

"I did tell you—I got locked out in the rain."

"Not *that*!"

I didn't follow her. Azra and Wen were the only ones I'd told anything about what happened at the wedding. After everything that had happened to me since that horrible weekend, I was trying not to think too much about any of it. I was now trying a new strategy: complete denial.

In artistically placed blobs, I plopped the jelly onto another slice of bread. "What are you talking about, Azra?"

"You know—oh, come on. Don't be like that. . . ."

"Like what? I have no idea what you mean. Isn't it a lovely day?"

I tenderly placed the bread with the blobs, on top of the bread with the happy face. Then I reached for the knife again so I could slice the sandwich in half. Richard liked his sandwiches cut diagonally.

Over the phone I could hear Azra blowing air like she was losing her patience. "That guy . . . the poet? The one with the girlfriend? You never told me everything that happened." When I still didn't say anything, she said,

"About when you danced with him?" And then her voice suddenly got low and secretive. "You know, about how you and he were on the sofa with your hand on his rear end?"

I hacked the sandwich in one quick barbaric chop.

It felt like a bomb had gone off.

If word was out about this, my life as I knew it was over.

"Floey? Are you there?"

Abandoning Richard's sandwich, I ran with the phone into my room and shut the door. "How did you find out about that?"

"Leslie told me. She heard it from Kate." Kate was another JC.

"What? How would Kate know?"

"I don't know. She wouldn't say."

This was not good. If somebody had somehow found out about the whole Calvin incident, if people now knew about it, I would forever be known as the tramp who squeezed the butt of the Zen cowboy.

There was probably no way to live something like that down.

"What do you mean she wouldn't say?"

"Leslie walked home with her today and Kate told her it's what she heard from somebody, but she wouldn't tell her who. She said it would be betraying a confidence."

"What!"

"Leslie told me, but she figured I already knew because, you know, because you and I are best friends and everything."

"Oh my God, Azra! This is terrible!"

"Then it's true?"

"You have to tell me who knows about this!"

"I'm not sure. Could be a lot of people, but maybe not. Leslie, Kate and whoever told her. And me, of course. I only heard about it just now."

"Floey!" Richard shouted from the office. He was glued to the computer again. *"Where's my sandwich!"*

For a moment I wondered if Richard could have been the leak, but he hadn't been in the same room as Calvin and me, so he didn't know anything about what had happened.

"Tell me everything. What did you say? What did *he* say?"

The room was spinning around me. "Please . . . please don't tell anyone. Tell Leslie and Kate not to tell anybody else either, okay?"

"Okay, okay. But tell me, are you, like, seeing him now or anything? Does that Melanie girl know? Is that why you've been acting so weird?"

"Hurry up, Floey!"

"No, I'm not seeing him, Azra. I have to go."

I set down the phone without saying goodbye.

Richard looked irritated when I brought him his sandwich. Under normal circumstances I might have said something like "Why are you still here?" or "Have you started packing yet?" or something equally witty, but my mind was reeling. I just handed him his plate and left the room. I was trying to understand what could have happened. There were only three people who had seen me dancing with Calvin at the wedding: Lillian, Rebecca Greenblatt and Aunt Sarah. Lillian was on her honeymoon and Aunt Sarah was in Alaska. Rebecca might have said something, but I didn't think it was her. How would something Rebecca said get to Kate Bates? But then I remembered that Kate used to go to Moses Brown until she was kicked out because her grades were so bad. Then I remembered that her older brother still went there.

Just like Calvin.

I wasn't sure if Kate's brother was a poet too, but I vaguely remembered hearing that he read a lot. He and Calvin were probably friends. The most likely person to have blabbed about what happened between Calvin and me was Calvin himself. That had to be it. It made perfect sense.

I ran to my room and grabbed a pen and a blank sheet of paper. My fingers couldn't write as fast as the angry words burned through my mind. I'd crumpled up a few sheets before I was satisfied enough to send it, which I did immediately. I didn't know Calvin's address but figured that the main office at Moses Brown would know where to find him.

Dear Calvin,

I hope you and your Cro-Magnon buddies are happy. You must have felt like such a big man showing off about how you got a thirteen-year-old drunk and then embarrassed her in front of her own family! What an impressive accomplishment! I bet you and your friends laughed pretty hard. I bet you scratched yourselves, pounded your chests and grunted like the testosterone-fueled cavemen you really are. But I just thought you should know: now that word is out about that night, my life is completely ruined. I'll never be able to look my friends or family in the face again. I hope it was worth it to you, you big skinny unenlightened fake.

Very sincerely,
Floey Packer

P.S. I also hope you realize I will never ever forgive you as long as I live!!

• • •

Soon after that, I caught three different people leering at me.

It started that afternoon at the studio when a kid with glasses got his picture taken with his Saint Bernard. Gary had gone to the bathroom, probably to adjust his comb-over, so I got to set up the boy and the dog. They were wearing matching sweaters. The weird thing was, the kid seemed a little scared of me. He wouldn't make eye contact but I felt his eyes follow me around the room. It was really creepy. And then when I leaned over to adjust his position, I caught him staring down my blouse! What kind of lowlife sneaks a peek at the photographer's assistant's boobs? So I gave him the most hateful stare I could. He turned white and pretended he was looking at something behind me, so I carried on with what I was doing.

Then when I left to go home it happened again. Outside the door, a couple of kids about Richard's age stopped talking when I came out. While I unlocked my bike they pretended they weren't watching me, but I turned my head quickly and caught them. My heart started racing and I know I blushed.

When I was a little way down the road, I looked over my shoulder again. They were still watching.

Tuesday, July 8, 3:35 p.m.

Dear Insightful Floey,

Is it my imagination or does something about me attract little boys? What is it that makes me so fascinating to them and invisible to everybody else? Is it possible that a story Calvin told could get all the way to these kids? Are Leslie and Kate complete blabbermouths? Do they have absolutely no sense of decency? Or does Richard really have that picture? Has he hung it up somewhere? Oh God!

I called Azra to find out if she'd heard anything else about Calvin. She hadn't. I asked if she'd heard anybody say they saw my picture. She hadn't. So I told her about the boys. Was I being ridiculous? She didn't think so.

"That happens to Leslie and me all the time," she said. "It's a guy thing. They pretty much spend their entire lives sneaking looks at us."

"They do?"

"You didn't know that? God, Floey, even after your little thing with that cowboy, you're still so innocent! Leslie and Kate and I talk about this all the time. Girls are about the only thing guys ever think about. That's why boys in passing cars shout out their windows at us. That never happens to guys. It's not fair, but it's the way it is."

"But these are little kids, nine or maybe ten years old," I said, ignoring the crack about me being innocent.

"Doesn't matter. Leslie says they're all the same. They think it's funny. Leslie has three brothers, so she ought to know."

I took a deep breath. Usually I didn't hide it when I got mad at Azra, but now, hearing her talk as if Leslie were her best friend instead of me, I didn't say anything. I didn't want her to know how hurt I felt.

All I could think to say was "What about Wen?"

"Him too, I'm sure."

She'd certainly become the expert on worldly matters. I supposed that was what came from being a day-camp junior counselor. I, on the other hand, didn't think I'd ever understand boys.

Tuesday, July 8, 4:05 p.m.

I'm sitting in the anjali mudra position, legs crossed, back aligned, chin pulled in. Just because the world is full of creeps and crazies, that doesn't mean I have to let it affect my journey to enlightenment. Deep breaths. I'm envisioning the relationship between my posture, breath and mind. I'm becoming one with everything. . .

Wait, that reminds me of a joke.

This Zen master goes up to a hot dog stand and says, "Make me one with everything." Ha!

But there's more: So the hot dog vendor gives him his hot dog, takes his money and puts it into a box. After a moment, the Zen master says, "Where's my change?" but the hot dog vendor just stares at him and says, "Change must come from within."

Ha!

Oh, typical! Ma just came in and told me to stop wasting the whole day in my room making weird noises and get outside and enjoy the sunshine. She's about as unenlightened as they come.

My mother gave me a list of groceries to pick up and told me I had to bring Tish along. Since Tish didn't have a bicycle, we had to walk. First, though, I had to wait while she made herself a Fluffernutter sandwich. She offered to make me one, but I said no. I decided to try to subtly help her see how bad it was for her, so I told her that instead of eating it I might as well rub the sandwich directly onto my butt since that was where it would end up anyway.

As usual, she didn't take the hint.

Billy Fishman was sitting on his lawn with a couple of his henchmen. I wasn't sure where Richard was. Their eyes followed us as we walked up the street. When we were almost at his house Billy called out to me.

"Hi, Floey," he said in that squeaky voice of his. "Did you have fun at the barbecue? Everything certainly seemed to go off with a *bang*! You sure showed your *sparkling* personality!"

The little boys giggled.

"What you did with that firecracker wasn't funny," I said. "I ought to pop you one right now."

"No need to get *explosive*!"

It's amazing how much difference two years can make in terms of maturity. Compared to me, these boys were like babies. I kept walking. I didn't feel like getting into a big thing with Billy Fishman.

"Shut up, Billy," Tish said. But she wasn't looking at him. She kept her eyes down.

He laughed. "Careful eating that sandwich. You might get overexcited and bite off your own fingers."

"Grow up," she said.

Billy said something back to her, but it was quiet. His friends laughed pretty hard. I wasn't sure I'd heard it right, but it sounded like he called her something mean. From Tish's face I could tell she'd heard it.

Now, the Old Floey would have kept walking. But I decided that the New Floey should be different. Maybe Tish wasn't my favorite person in the world, but she was my cousin and Billy shouldn't talk to her that way. The New Floey, I decided, stood up to bullies.

So I stopped and turned around. "What did you say?"

"Never mind," Tish said. "Let's go."

"No," I said. "He said something. What was it?"

Billy just grinned.

"Whatever it was, I bet you wouldn't say it again."

Slowly, he stood up. I immediately realized I'd made a terrible mistake. Somehow, I'd forgotten just how big Billy was.

"Sure I would. I called her Chunky Monkey," he said, taking a step toward me. "What are you going to do about it?"

Suddenly, I wasn't so sure I wanted to do anything about it. Was I actually going to get into a fight with Gorilla Boy? I'd like to say that I stared him down, that it didn't matter that he stood at least a head taller than me. I'd like to say that I stood my ground and told him to take back what he'd said to Tish.

But that would be a lie.

A couple of Billy's friends stood up too, and the others sat up on the grass. Like me, they could sense a fight coming. Billy took another step forward. My heart was beating fast and I felt sick to my stomach. I wondered how vomiting on Billy might work as a battle tactic.

"Come on," Tish said, tugging at my arm. "It doesn't matter, let's just go."

That was all I needed to hear to turn and walk away. The New Floey might have been brave and honorable, I told myself, but she wasn't stupid.

Tish and I never mentioned that little incident again.

• • •

Wednesday when I went to get my diary, I noticed that something was wrong.

The socks I hid it under seemed almost right, but not quite. One of my yellows stuck out just a little too far. I hadn't left it like that.

Somebody had disturbed my pile.

They had probably found my diary.

Maybe even read it.

I didn't need to think especially hard to guess who it was. I was furious. Didn't Richard and Tish have consciences? Didn't they have a clue about right and wrong? As soon as Ma came back from the mall with them, I was going to explain my secret clothing pile to her and let her go wild on them. The New Floey had been patient and forgiving up until now, but this time they had crossed a sacred line.

That's when the phone rang.

"You better come over and see this," Wen's voice said. It sounded urgent.

"Wen, you have no idea what my cousins did to me. I'm so mad I can hardly talk."

"Did you hear me?" he asked.

"No. See what?"

"Uh . . . I really think it's better if you see for yourself. You should probably come over here right away."

"Don't do this to me, Wen," I said, trying to stay calm. On top of everything else, I still wasn't completely finished being mad at him. "What do you want to show me? Why are you acting so mysterious?" But when he wouldn't tell me anything more, I started to get worried, so I gave in. "Okay," I said, "I'll be over as soon as I can. But this better be good."

I set down the phone, closed my eyes and tried to project myself onto the beautiful Mexican beach from Lillian's postcard. I was standing up to my waist in the warm, clear water, looking back at the grass huts and white sand, a cool breeze moving my hair around just slightly, the smooth, soft sand squishing between my toes. I leaned back and let the water surround me and lift me up on its gentle waves under the warm blue sky so far, far away from Rhode Island.

What could be worse than having my diary invaded, my privacy violated? It was only July and already I couldn't wait for this horrible summer to end. My only comfort as I biked to Wen's house was the certainty that things couldn't possibly get worse.

Wrong.

chapterten: in which i discover the ugly truth

• • • • • • • • • • • •

"Okay," I demanded as soon as Wen opened the door. "So what is it?"

His face was a study in gloom and doom. "You're not going to be happy."

"If you think that's news, you don't have a clue what I've been living with for the past week and a half." But I could see from his eyes that he wasn't interested in hearing my story just then, so I stopped. "Why not?"

He put his hand into his pocket and pulled out a folded piece of paper. Without saying a word, he unfolded it. Then he held it up.

It was a full-color photocopy of the infamous birthday picture.

I actually screamed.

"This is the picture Azra sent to your aunt, isn't it?"

I blinked a few times to see if it would go away. It didn't. "Oh . . . my . . . God! Where did you get this?"

"I found it under George's bed."

"What? I'm going to kill Azra! This isn't funny!"

Wen looked at the picture again. "I don't know. I think it's kind of humorous. It's eye-catching, anyway." He was trying to make me feel better, but it wasn't working. How could anybody see any humor in this?

I snatched it out of his hand and glared at him.

"There's more," he said. "Look, there's a Web address at the bottom."

Penciled below the picture was "www.floeysprivate-life.com." The blood supply for the entire lower half of my body flooded into my face.

I screamed again.

Then I put my hands over my mouth and forced myself to stay calm. "So," I said, "what did George say when you found this?"

"He doesn't know. I only discovered it a little while ago. He's out somewhere with my dad."

The image was fuzzy. I could barely recognize it as me, but I knew it was. The bra was clearly too small. The cleavage was so obvious, I looked like Bubble Woman. What was I thinking, posing like that?

This was bad. Very bad.

"Turn on your computer, Wen. I have to see this Web site."

"You're not going to like it."

His computer was already on with the Web page glowing from the screen. Obviously, he'd already checked it out. I sat down. Somebody had cropped my head from the picture so my own ridiculous grinning face was beaming back at me. Written in big green flashing letters above my head was *IT'S FLOEY'S PRIVATE LIFE!* Below that was a button that read *ENTER*.

Horrified, I looked from the monitor to Wen and then back again.

This was beyond awful. It was absolutely, positively nuclear awful.

"Go on," Wen said quietly.

I clicked the button. The next screen showed two more pictures, one of me sitting on the front steps with Richard's fizzing firecracker, and the other of me wearing my Halloween costume—they'd scanned my shot and cropped out Wen and Azra. Incredibly, there was even a special offer: *Send $3 and get a special photo extra!* This must have been how George got the birthday picture.

But that wasn't the worst of it. Something caught in my throat when I saw the last link, the main attraction of the site by the size of the letters. It said, *DAILY DIARY ENTRY.*

"Oh . . . my . . . God."

I clicked it.

There it was for anybody to see: my private diary, my most personal, secret thoughts. It started with my thirteenth birthday and continued from there. Scanning ahead, I saw everything I'd written about Lillian's wedding, the incident with Calvin's butt, my cousins, the poetry reading—it went all the way up to my entry about Zen meditation. That was only the day before. God, it was all there, every humiliating detail of my life!

There was no question who had done this.

Yes, I'd been a little unfriendly to them at the beginning. Yes, I'd told them to stay out of my life and away from my private things just before searching through their stuff. But this was taking things way too far. This was way worse than anything else my cousins could have done to me.

I had to peek around my fingers because by then I'd covered my face. "How many people have read this, do you think?"

"I don't know."

"What am I going to do?"

He just shifted his weight behind me.

Were they *both* involved? I felt upset enough about Richard, but for some reason I felt even more betrayed by Tish. Lately I'd almost started to think that she wasn't the demon he was. But it didn't matter now. Only one thing was certain: the Web site had to come down, and the sooner the better.

And then I suddenly remembered everything I'd written about Wen. I realized with horror that he might already have read every embarrassing word. He was still shifting his weight back and forth behind me. I couldn't bring myself to turn around and face him.

I jumped out of the chair and ran for the door.

"Where are you going, Floey?"

"Home!"

• • •

I pedaled as hard as I could. The wind whipped my hair back. When I reached my house our car still wasn't in the driveway, but I threw open the front door anyway and looked around. There was nobody in the living room except Frank Sinatra, whose expression changed from bored to terrified as soon as he saw me. He jumped off the sofa and ran out of the room.

Great, even the ferret hated me now.

Nobody in the kitchen, the TV room, the bedrooms, the office or the basement. I checked out my window. Nobody in the backyard, either.

Then I saw the note on the kitchen table: *2:00 p.m.: Floey, Stopped by to see if you were here but you're out. I'm taking the children to Roger Williams Park Zoo. Chinese takeout tonight?—Love, Ma.*

I dropped down onto the kitchen floor and held my head in my hands. I had an awful vision of Calvin reading the letter I'd sent him. On top of feeling embarrassed about the Web site and everything I'd written about Azra and about Wen, now I was feeling new pangs of guilt. I'd accused an innocent man.

That's when I heard Wen's voice from outside. "Floey?"

At first I didn't move, but when I didn't hear anything else I knew he was still there, waiting for me. Eventually I walked to the screen door. He stared back at me from the bottom of the steps.

"Are you okay?" he said finally.

I shook my head.

He stayed on his bike, straddling the crossbar. "Listen, do you want to go to the secret beach? We could talk."

I shook my head again. I didn't want to go anywhere. All I wanted to do was slip back into the wallpaper. Or maybe crawl under a rock.

"I'm too humiliated to talk right now," I said almost under my breath. "Please go away."

But he still didn't leave. We both waited through an awkward silence that seemed to go on for hours. What had I been I thinking, writing all that stuff down? Why did I keep a diary at all? I wondered if anything this bad had ever happened to anybody else. Ever.

And how long was Wen going to stay down there looking at me?

Finally, I asked him the question that I dreaded the most. "How much . . . ," I began. I had a hard time getting the words out. "How much did you read?"

The look in his eyes said everything.

"Some of it. Enough."

I felt like hiding under the sofa.

"I guess I was a jerk and didn't even know it," he said. "I'm sorry." When I didn't answer he said, "Look, Floey, you don't need to be embarrassed. You *know* I really like you too. We're buddies. You said it yourself right in your own diary, you'd hate to ruin our friendship. I'm glad you wouldn't want that to change. And you wouldn't, right?"

Cautiously, I shook my head.

"So I agree, that's the best way. We're friends and we shouldn't screw it up. That's good, isn't it?"

I still didn't know what to say, so I just said, "I guess so."

He set down his bike, came up the steps and stood on

the other side of the screen. "You going to let me in, or are you coming out?"

After another long moment he opened the door and took my hand, and then we sat down together on the top step. He was wearing his black high-tops, the ones I liked. He massaged the back of my neck. "Besides, if you're the wallpaper, you'd probably be better off with someone else, the carpet or the window or somebody like that. Oh, but I forgot, you're all new now."

Whatever he was doing to my neck, it felt good so I let him keep doing it for a while. I almost smiled. Almost.

"So," I said, glancing sideways at him, "what are *you*, then?"

"Me? Oh, Floey of the Miserable Present, I'm surprised you need to ask me that." He stopped rubbing my neck so he could pretend to look shocked. "I'm Bugle Boy, remember?"

He smiled and then I smiled and suddenly everything seemed almost okay.

Almost.

We stared down at our shoes, not saying anything. Eventually he put his arm around my shoulder. "Hey, things may look bad now . . ."

For the first time in this whole conversation I looked directly at him. I could see my face reflected in the glare of his glasses. "Bad, Wen? My life is ruined. My diary is up on the World Wide Web, for God's sake. Who even knows how many ten-year-olds out there are regular readers?"

He nodded. "I guess you're right. It's just horrible."

"No, this isn't 'just horrible' either. There isn't a word horrible enough for what this is."

"You've got to admit," he said, "there's a side of it that's pretty funny." And then he started laughing. I'm not sure what he was laughing at, but whatever it was he certainly thought it was hilarious.

I socked him hard in the shoulder and he cried out. "Owwww!"

And then, out of nowhere, I started laughing too. I'd been feeling like everything was just so terrible for so long, maybe there was a part of me that was getting tired of it. I'm not sure. What I *do* know is that sitting on my front steps, Wen and I laughed pretty hard, and after that I felt a little better.

And that's when an amazing new plan suddenly came to me. It was something ridiculous, something that the plain old unexceptional Floey would *never* have done in a *million* years.

"Listen," I said, sitting up. "I might have an idea. It's a little crazy. Want to hear it?"

He shook his head, still laughing. "No, not really."

I ignored him. "How about if I let the Web site stay up?"

He stopped laughing and gave me a sideways glance like I was crazy.

Maybe I was.

But there's a Zen saying: When cold, be thoroughly cold; when hot, be hot through and through.

"Wait, listen! My cousins don't know that I know they're reading my diary and putting it online, right? So, what if I keep writing as if nothing had happened—except starting now I *make things up*?"

"What are you talking about?"

"When blogging, blog."

He looked at me like I'd just sprouted a new nose.

"Look, I can't do anything about what already happened, but this could be an opportunity to turn the tables on them. What could I write that would embarrass an eleven-year-old boy or a ten-year-old girl?"

"Floey, that would be kind of mean."

I smiled. "Exactly."

He rolled his eyes. "So the New Floey is a writer now? Making up stories?"

I grinned.

"Your problem is that this New Floey is completely deranged."

I nodded. It was a deranged idea.

But they definitely deserved it.

• • •

When Richard, Tish and my mother finally came home, I didn't mention a thing. Later that night, I pulled out my diary, as usual. After I finished writing, I placed it back in my drawer, careful to bury it beneath my socks and underwear.

chaptereleven: in which i become a writer

• • • • • • • • • • • •

Wednesday, July 9, 11:00 p.m.

My Dearest Floey,

Why can't Richard stop picking his nose? He's always at it! Last night I caught him again while we were watching television. He sank his finger in two knuckles deep, dug around awhile and then pulled out a fat, wet booger you could have put on a hook and used as bait. He didn't look away from the TV, not even for a second. So gross! He does it so often I'm not even sure he knows he's doing it, the little snot-miner. So there he was, staring bug-eyed at a car chase while his finger and thumb rolled the thing back and forth until it got all rubbery. Eventually he wiped it on his pants. After that he moved on to the other nostril but this time the booger he pulled out had a long liquidy tail that hung on, so he rubbed it off with his knuckle. Hasn't anyone ever taught him about tissues?

God! We were eating popcorn! I will never eat anything out of the same bowl as that little piggy ever again!!

Even Wen laughed when I read it to him. If Tish could write stories, so could I. Okay, so maybe I enhanced the truth just a little, but that's a writer's prerogative.

When Wen and I looked it up on floeysprivatelife.com the next day, there was just a short note saying that I'd skipped writing in my journal that night. I had this hilarious image of Richard and Tish reading what I'd written and then the discussion between them about whether it should be included on the Web page.

My next masterpiece went like this:

<u>Thursday, July 10, 2:10 p.m.</u>

Dear Floey,

I feel so guilty. Last night by mistake I used the wrong toothbrush and today my canker sores are back. My doctor says canker sores are very VERY contagious. This time I have one under my tongue and another on the inside of my lower lip. Boy, are they painful! I would say something but I'm not sure whose toothbrush I used. Besides, I'm too embarrassed. Anyway, I'm not sure there's anything they could do about it.

Oh well. What they don't know won't hurt them, I guess.

Later, I heard Tish in the bathroom gargling.

In the early afternoon I passed the two of them sitting at the kitchen table. They were snacking again. I went over to the refrigerator, pulled out a can of soda and opened it up. After taking a long sip I made a point of putting my hand to my lip and wincing with imaginary pain. Then I held the can out to them.

"I don't think I can drink this. Do either of you want to finish it?"

They both looked revolted. They shook their heads.

"That's a shame," I said. I left the can between them on the table and walked away.

• • •

Azra called. Even though I'd wanted to phone her first so we could talk about the things I'd written, I hadn't because I was scared about what she would say. So I'd tried not to think about it—denial again. The day I found out about floeysprivatelife.com it had even crossed my mind to ask Wen not to tell her about it, but in the end I didn't. So I figured she had almost surely heard about it from him.

"That's some Web site you've got there, Floey," she said, her voice not as friendly as usual.

"It's not exactly *mine,* but thanks, I guess." After a long, weird silence I asked, "Are you mad at me?"

"Why? Because you haven't called in almost three days? Because you didn't tell me about the site yourself? Or do you mean because you think I'm Leslie Dern's lapdog?"

"I don't really think you're her lapdog," I said. "At the time I was just a little annoyed. . . ."

"And I'm a follower? I wouldn't stand out even in an empty room?"

I cringed. "I write a lot of stupid ideas in my diary. That's all it was. You have to believe me. I was just venting. I didn't really mean any of it."

"No? You didn't? Then why did you write it?"

"I . . . don't know. I'm so sorry, Azra. I feel just terrible."

"But that's not even the worst of it. How about when you wrote about trying to make Wen your boyfriend? Didn't you mean that either?"

I closed my eyes.

There was another long silence. I knew that what I had written about Wen was really the biggest reason she was mad. We had an agreement. Once again I felt my stomach move around and I wondered if I was going to puke. Azra was my best friend. Would she ever even talk to me again?

That's when she hung up.

I dropped my head onto the kitchen table with no intention of ever lifting it. I wanted everyone I had ever met to hate me forever. I deserved it.

After a few minutes, I tried calling her back. Thankfully, she picked it up. "I'm really, really sorry, Azra."

I heard her take a deep breath. "I know you are," she said, sounding a little calmer than before. "I've been thinking about it. I guess I was the one who started it by calling you ordinary. I didn't mean that either."

"Really?" I said, surprised. "So you forgive me?"

She didn't answer right away. Finally she said, "Look, I don't want us to fight. I, your unremarkable friend, might be willing to forgive you—but only if you swear that you didn't mean it, and that you forgive me for what I said to you on your birthday."

"I do. I swear."

I could almost hear her relax. "When I was seven," she said, trying to laugh, "I used to keep a diary. I found it last year and I couldn't even *believe* some of the things I wrote."

But I still didn't feel like we were finished yet. "And all that stuff about Wen? You're okay with that?"

"Floey, we've been best friends since second grade. You think I don't know that you wish we hadn't made that deal? I guess we all have our own little moments of insanity, right? But in the end I know you'd never really break it. I trust you."

Now I felt even guiltier. Six years of friendship meant a lot. I was suddenly more determined than ever that Wen and I should never be more than friends.

"I'm glad," I said, my heart beating again. "I'm so glad. You really are remarkable, Azra, you know that? You definitely stand out from the crowd."

"You bet I do," she said.

After that I felt a lot better. We talked about the Web site and I told her about the fake diary entries. Azra thought I was crazy. But not so crazy that she didn't laugh—and come up with an idea of her own. This one was about Wen and Tish.

Friday, July 11, 11:30 a.m.

Dear Ms. Packer,

Wen's been acting peculiar lately. He's in his own world half the time. Sometimes when I talk to him he barely pays any attention at all. And whenever I mention Tish he gets all flustered and goofy. So I asked him about it. At first he didn't want to say anything, but I finally got him to admit it—he has a crush on her! Can you believe it? He can't get her out of his head! He says he's confused about it because, for one thing, he doesn't know if she likes him. For another, he's not sure how he feels about getting into a winter-spring romance. Besides, he knows she'll be going back to Chicago soon, so he doesn't feel right about saying anything to her. I'd better not mention it. It wouldn't be right for me to get involved. I wonder if he'll ever let her know his true feelings?

To be honest, I didn't really think this one would work. If it did, it was pretty mean since Tish actually had a crush on Wen—that was obvious even to Azra, so her idea was just to add fuel to the fire. After what Tish and Richard had done to me, though, I felt okay going through with it.

When we told Wen about today's as-yet-unpublished diary entry, he didn't think it was funny. "That poor girl," he said. "You shouldn't play with her that way. She's only ten."

He was right, and I immediately felt sorry.

Not.

The next day, Wen called and Tish happened to pick up the phone. According to Wen, as soon as she heard his voice, her voice dropped down to a whisper. "Listen, Wen. I have something I want to say to you."

"Uh . . . okay," he said.

"I've been getting the idea that you might have . . . feelings for me."

"Oh, Tish, I—"

"Please, don't say anything until I'm finished. Don't ask me how I know, but I know. Sometimes a woman can just tell these things. If it really is true, then I want you to know that as flattered as I am, it could never work out. I'm too young for you. You need to find someone your own age. Please don't take this the wrong way."

Wen said he wasn't sure what to say, so there was a long pause before he finally said, "Okay."

"I'm trying to let you down as gently as I can."

"Thank you."

"I'll go get Floey now."

"Thanks."

• • •

Unfortunately, Tish is a smart girl and wasn't fooled for long.

"Floey," she whispered to me from the other bed. "Are you asleep?"

It was late Saturday night and I was wide awake. I made my voice sound groggy. "Why do you have to keep waking me up every night? Are you trying to torture me?"

Her bed squeaked. "The things you've been writing in your diary—you're making them all up."

I turned my head. From the moonlight shining through my window I could just about see her eyes peering over at me. It wasn't a question. She said it like she knew it was a fact.

I glared across the room at her. "So you're actually *admitting* that you read my diary?"

She nodded. "It doesn't matter. You already know anyway."

"Well, aren't you Miss Clever."

She didn't answer.

"Tish, didn't you ever think about what an awful thing you were doing? So much bad karma? Didn't it occur to you how mean it was to put somebody's diary up on the Internet? Not to mention sending out that picture. It's all so . . . well, it's unforgivable! What's wrong with you?"

"It wasn't me," she said calmly.

"No? You're just sweet and innocent, are you? Innocently reading my diary?"

She was quiet for a long time. "I don't blame you for being mad," she said finally. "I'd be mad if I were you. Even though they told me not to, I was still going to tell you. You just found out first."

"Sure you were," I said, trying to keep my voice quiet. "Okay then, so if it wasn't you, who was it?"

"Richard, but don't be too mad at him. He's being used."

And then the whole ugly story spilled out.

According to Tish, it was Billy's idea to look through the diary. She said that the first day they played with Billy and his friends in the street, Billy had a pair of binoculars. He told them he used them to watch me from his bedroom window before I'd started being more careful to close the shades. Fortunately for me, the most he'd ever seen though my window was me in my nightshirt reading or writing. At least, that's what he told them. That's when Richard told Billy that he knew what I must have been writing. The diary.

"I whispered to him to shut up, but he didn't listen," Tish said.

"I bet you did."

She ignored me and continued. So the next thing was that Billy told my cousins that he and his friends had started a spy club. He said that they could join, but first they needed to find the diary and bring it out to them. "I wouldn't do it," Tish said. "And at first, Richard wasn't going to either, but he really wanted to be Billy's friend."

"So you guys just decided it was okay to search my room?"

"I told you it wasn't me, it was Richard. But you were really mean to us, Floey, lording it over us and yelling at us to stay out of everything. You made it hard *not* to want to go through your things. Plus you went through Richard's stuff, right?"

I didn't say anything.

"Besides, if you were going to wave your diary around and bully us about reading it, then you should've found a better hiding place than your sock drawer."

I glared at her in the darkness. "Well . . . go on!"

"So he brought the diary out. He wanted to be part of the gang. It's hard for him to make friends, you know. He's really shy. And sometimes," she added, her voice dropping to an even lower whisper, "he can even be kind of unsociable."

Big news flash.

The next day, Tish said, Richard tried to get Billy and his friends interested in something else, so he told them it could be fun if they started a computer game Web site together. Unfortunately, Billy liked the Web site idea, but not for computer games.

And thus, floeysprivatelife.com was born.

According to Tish, Richard had also made the mistake of mentioning the birthday picture to Billy. It had been in his pocket the day I'd searched his room. That gave Billy the idea of the special photo extra, so they could even make a little money.

Pretty soon, my Web site had a following. In just a few short days, not only were the boys on the street reading the daily updates, but some of their buddies in town and in other nearby towns were even in on it.

"The spy club is all Billy and his friends ever talk about now," Tish whispered. "Everybody just goes along with whatever Billy wants, including Richard, even though I know he feels guilty about it. I told him he's a jerk for doing it. I've been staying out of it and that's why they don't want to play with me."

"So this club, do they spy on anybody other than me?"

Tish shook her head. "But they don't know that you know, and I'm not going to tell them either."

By this time I was lying down on my bed again, staring back up at the ceiling. I wasn't sure what to believe. If Aunt Sarah thought *I* was a bad influence, I wondered what she'd have thought of her own *son* if she knew?

"You'd be surprised how big a fan club you have," Tish whispered solemnly. "You're kind of a star."

• • •

The next morning I noticed that floeysprivatelife.com's audience was getting bigger. Richard had added a message board for people to write comments about the Web pages and about me. To get in, readers now needed to buy their own password (Tish gave me Richard's, which was "enlightenment"—he planned to change them every few days) and there was a growing list of names, with messages from people in Providence, Newport, and even some from Chicago. Who were these people? Some of the messages were mean, like the one that congratulated Wen for "dodging the bullet," or the one that called me a "hopeless airhead." But a lot of them were nicer, like the one from the guy who hoped I came out of my depression because I had a lot to offer. There were even a bunch of really surprising postings that said I was pretty—actually, they used words like "hot" and "built" and, my favorite, "lovely Venus." This was all pretty scary, but in a bizarre way it was also kind of flattering. Sure, these were the comments of a bunch of perverts, but still, I began looking at myself in a new way. Suddenly I wasn't the wallpaper anymore. I felt more like a chandelier (if you know what I mean), or maybe a fountain.

Even Lillian had never had her own Web site.

That afternoon I thought of a way to put my new publishing power to more practical use. Ma had been bugging me to cut the grass, along with a long list of other chores she wanted me to do. So this is what I wrote:

Sunday, July 13, 1:40 p.m.

Dear oh dear,

I'm so frustrated! I really need a tan and I'd really love to go lie out in the sun in my tiny new bikini, but I don't know when I'll ever get the chance! Ma told me this week I have to:

1) Mow the lawn
2) Shake the dust out of all the rugs in the house
3) Straighten up the garage
4) Clean up all Richard's and Tish's stuff
5) Clean the bathroom
6) Give Frank Sinatra a bath

But it's pouring out now and it's supposed to rain every day this week except tomorrow, so that's probably the only chance I'll get. Too bad

I'll have to waste it doing chores. It's so disappointing!

Of course, there was only a small part of me that really thought Richard's army of little perverts might actually do my work just so they could get a picture of me sunning myself in a bikini I didn't really own.

But the power of the Internet surprised me.

The next day turned out to be clear and beautiful. Soon after my mother left the house to play doubles with Gary, the doorbell rang. It was Billy and three of his friends.

"Hi, Floey. We're trying to make some extra money and were wondering if you have any work you'd like us to do for you around the house."

I smiled.

A moment later, I stood over them as one boy started up the lawn mower and the others pulled apart the pile of junk in the garage and repacked it in neat order. They dragged the rugs down the front steps and shook big clouds of dust out of them. And then there was poor Frank Sinatra. My mother hadn't really asked me to give him a bath, but I was still mad at him for being unfaithful, so I'd added him to my list. It took two of the braver boys to hold him still. He made long, eerie ferret moans while they hosed him down and worked the shampoo into his fur. Pathetic and annoyed, he peered out at me as if he knew I was to blame.

They worked cheap. I only had to take a few dollars out of the cash my mother kept in the cookie jar. Interestingly,

Richard didn't help his friends. In fact, he seemed uncomfortable that they were knocking themselves out for me. He cleaned his room himself (Tish did ours) and then he took a walk.

Floeysprivatelife.com was out of his control.

Tish, who was hanging around me the whole time she wasn't cleaning, kept looking over at me and giggling. When the boys finished up in the bathroom I was on the living room sofa and Tish was lying on the floor flipping through one of her magazines. I was starting a new book that the librarian had suggested, *Live in a Better Way: Reflections on Truth, Love and Happiness* by the Dalai Lama. The Dalai Lama says people can train their minds to be happier. Even though I liked the idea, I didn't really get how you could actually do it.

The boys marched into the room wearing rubber gloves and big silly grins. "All done!" they said. "It's a beautiful day. Perfect for lying out in the sun, don't you think?"

I raised my eyes from the page only for a moment. "No, not today," I said. "I think I'm just going to stay in and read. But I sure do appreciate your help!"

Tish had a hard time controlling herself. She pretended she was having a coughing fit and had to leave the room.

If only I had a picture of their disappointed faces. How I would have liked to upload *that*!

• • •

Over the next few days, I had that spy club running around in circles. One afternoon I wrote that I particularly like boys who wear bike shorts. The next morning, as the crowd of boys watched me pedal past on my way to Gary's, I noticed that two or three of them were sporting tight spandex shorts with padded behinds.

I admit it. I was enjoying my new life.

By Wednesday I was fussing more than usual in front of the mirror. I spent a long time deciding on outfits. Should I try to look slimmer in my black capris and my red and black striped blouse, or instead should I go with a plain white T-shirt and blue jean cutoffs? As long as people were watching me, I wanted to make a good impression.

Even my mother noticed.

"Are you trying to impress Wen?" she asked, stopping to watch me from the end of the hallway.

"No, Ma," I said, blushing.

"Then who is he?"

"I just want to look my best. What's wrong with that?" There was no way she could have understood that I was constantly in the spotlight. I didn't want to disappoint my audience.

"Nothing. I'm just afraid if you stand in front of that mirror any longer, you're going to wear it out."

• • •

Having written in a diary every day since I was nine, I now found that I couldn't go long without writing something honest. So when I noticed that the Web site completely skipped over the three days before I'd bought my new hardcover diary, I was happy to realize that Richard didn't know about the spiral notebook. I'd never bothered to hide it, so he never read it. Since the hardcover diary was now my place for creative writing, the spiral notebook became my place for recording my *real* thoughts.

That Wednesday night, I had a lot to write about. Just when things had seemed to be getting so much better, they suddenly took a turn for the whole lot worse.

Wednesday, July 16, 9:15 p.m.

Dear Future Floey,

I absolutely cannot believe it! Ma has finally proven beyond any doubt that she doesn't give a flying fart about me! Without even asking my opinion she just goes ahead and agrees to let Aunt Sarah leave her kids with us for an EXTRA WHOLE WEEK LONGER than they were supposed to stay!! They'll be here until the 26th, the day after Lillian comes back!! Apparently, the support group ladies are finding out so much about themselves that some of them have signed up for an extra adventure—this one involves five days kayaking through a fjord! I don't see why I should have to keep putting up with her rotten children just because Aunt Sarah wants to freeze her sour butt off on some glacier! Of course, when I say that to Ma, she refuses to listen. Then when I point out that I hardly seem to matter around here, that she doesn't seem to notice me or care about me, she tells me to stop being childish. Childish! So that's when I say, "Did you know that Wen dumped me almost three weeks ago?" and she says, "No. Why didn't you tell me?" So I say, "You never asked! You never even noticed that I've been incredibly depressed!" So then she goes all quiet and eventually says how sorry she is but it's been a really busy time. I don't say anything. I just leave her and lock myself here in the bathroom again.

So now I'm stuck with my alien cousins until ten whole days from now—that is, assuming Aunt Sarah ever really does bother to come back. With my luck she'll get herself eaten by a polar bear and her kids will end up living here permanently!

The next night, my mother announced that she was taking me out to dinner, just the two of us. Of course, right away I recognized this for what it was: a blatant attempt to make up for her appalling lack of awareness about my life. I told her no thanks. She wasn't getting off the hook that easily. But then she told me she'd arranged for Richard and Tish to go across to our neighbor Mrs. Horowitz for the evening, and that she'd made reservations at Cassarino's in Providence. It was my favorite restaurant and she knew it. I still wouldn't have gone, though, except then she brought out the clincher:

"And for after dinner," she said, "I rented us a movie. . . ."

"You did?" I asked, reluctantly looking up from a biography of Dogen Zenji, a Japanese Zen master from the thirteenth century.

She held up the box. It was *Change of Habit*. In this one, Elvis is an inner-city doctor who falls in love with Mary Tyler Moore, who falls in love with him, too. Unfortunately for them both, she's actually an undercover nun.

One more relationship down the tubes.

I couldn't say no. It was another one of our favorites.

• • •

In the mail the next day there was an envelope with what looked like Japanese writing printed on the edge.

Dear Floey,

I'm sorry somebody found out about the wedding, but you should know that I kept my promise to you. I haven't said a word to anybody. The worst part of this is that you may not believe me. I'd hate to think that you don't like me.

Here's a haiku I wrote about you:

bright and wild like fire
suddenly she steps forward
out of gray nothing

I'd like to read your poems. If you can stop hating me, please send some to me.

Your friend, Calvin

Dear Calvin,

sorry—i was wrong
now i know it wasn't you
can you forgive me?

do you really think
we don't matter when compared
with the universe?

i sure hope we do—
if we are unimportant
why write anything?

thanks for the poem
thirteen words that made me smile
feel free to send more
—Floey

chapter twelve:

deep wild violet

• • • • • • • • • • • •

I'd already told Azra that I'd changed my mind about going to Dean Eagler's party. Not only had Dean himself invited me, but this would also be a perfect opportunity to unveil the new, extraordinary Floey Packer in a big way. In front of a large crowd of the coolest kids in town I could show off a more confident, more together, happier me than ever before.

But first, I needed to prepare myself. I had a new look in mind.

Sunday, July 20, 2:00 p.m.

Ma just completely FLIPPED OUT on me! How can she actually forbid me to leave my room until I'm twenty-one?! It's not like I'm the first person on earth to dye my hair! Anyway, it's too late now—it's already done. Tish helped. Doing it was kind of messy but now I'll definitely stand out. And it looks great!

My hair is officially Deep Wild Violet!

A little after ten o'clock that night I snuck out my window. Tish promised to stay up and make sure Ma didn't check on me, but I arranged my pillows under my blanket to make it look like I was sleeping, just in case. Earlier, I'd paid a visit to Lillian's favorite used clothing store and picked out just the right clothes—a bright yellow strapless dress, funky yellow pumps and a yellow felt hat with a purple flower sewn to the front. It was perfect. Only someone truly confident, truly extraordinary would wear it.

I had to carry my pumps in one hand and pedal my bicycle barefooted. In such a short dress, I was glad it was dark. Still, this would be my first high school party, so I was very excited. Dean Eagler's long driveway was packed with old cars. There were going to be even more people than I'd expected. By the time I finally reached the front door, my palms were sweating. Stepping over that threshold would be a symbolic moment, a public announcement of my new beginning. But what if nobody noticed? What if people looked right through me, like before?

Then I got a grip on myself. My hair was violet. They'd notice.

I took a deep breath, smiled my most self-confident smile and opened the door. What greeted me was a row of muscle T-shirts. It was a crowd of football players, shouting and laughing about God only knew what. I had to push through them to get by. When the wall of muscles noticed me, it quieted down a little. There aren't a lot of people with violet hair in my town. Could some of these guys even know about the Web site?

Doesn't matter, I decided. I pretended not to care.

I shoved my way deeper into the house. I could barely hear anything over the pounding music. Where was Azra, or Dean, or anybody I knew? I kept squeezing my way through the people. Outside in a big garden at the back of the house a bunch of kids my age stood around under the floodlights.

"Floey? Is that you?"

From the other end of the crowded yard, Leslie Dern weaved her way toward me with Kate Bates right behind her. The JCs.

Leslie put her hands to her thin, birdlike face and screamed. "*Aaaah!* Oh my God! What happened to your hair!" She stared at it for a long time and then screamed again. "It looks like you're wearing a blueberry pie!"

Kate just stood there openmouthed, blinking at me.

"You don't like it?" I asked, already losing my confidence.

They seemed unsure. Eventually, Kate just stammered, "It's . . . well, it's . . ."

But then Dean Eagler appeared between them. He looked good, all tanned and relaxed with his black hair slicked back, kind of the happy-go-lucky Elvis from *Fun in Acapulco*. He leaned in toward my head and put one arm on Leslie's shoulder, the other on Kate's.

"Floey," he said, staring in amazement. "Is that really . . . purple?"

I nodded. "Violet, actually."

He shook his head and grinned. "Damn, that's cool."

Then he stepped forward, wrapped his arms around me and lifted me up. "I'm so glad you made it!"

"Thanks!" I said, relieved, and surprised that my feet no longer touched the ground. I tried to look over at the JCs but I couldn't turn my head that far with Dean squishing me. "Great party!" I shouted into his shirt.

He set me down and I shot a quick glance behind me. Leslie and Kate were bug-eyed, obviously amazed that Dean Eagler knew me.

"You still have that cold?" he asked.

"No," I said. "But thanks for asking." Wow, did he have sexy lips! "Dean, I'd like you to meet my friends Leslie and Kate."

"Yeah?" He hardly even glanced at them. "Nice to meet you."

And then he took my hand, squeezed it and gave me another one of his killer smiles. "Gotta go hang with my boys for a minute, but I'll come find you later."

"No problem," I said. "I'll see you when I see you."

He curled his lip again and left us. Kate's and Leslie's mouths hung open so wide I could practically see their tonsils. It was extremely satisfying.

Leslie leaned in close to me. "Your hair," she said seriously, "has to be the coolest thing I've ever seen in my whole life."

Kate nodded.

Suddenly, I liked them a little better. For the moment, I could almost forgive Leslie for trying to steal Azra.

Chalk one up for the extraordinary, visible New Floey Packer.

• • •

Alone again, I found Wen standing against the house, gazing toward the other side of the lawn. He stood out because he was wearing his loud Hawaiian shirt. I was glad to see him. I went over and put my hand on his arm.

"There you are," I said. "What are you looking at?"

He jumped. I guess I surprised him. When he saw it was me, he practically did a double take. "My God, Floey, what did you do?"

"It's just dye," I said casually. "Like it?"

He stared until I felt uncomfortable. Eventually he shrugged. "It's very New Floey, I guess."

I was a little disappointed. Of everybody I knew, I'd thought *Wen* would be the quickest to appreciate my new look. But since he didn't, I changed the subject. "You didn't answer my first question."

He nodded toward the back of the yard. "Look. What does that remind you of?"

I tried to see what he meant, but I didn't see anything except a dozen or so shadowy blobs moving around in the darkness beyond the floodlights. Soon, though, I realized these were people. Each blob was a couple making out in the grass.

"Remind me of? I don't know. What do they remind *you* of? And how long have you been gawking at them?"

"I'm not gawking," he said. "I'm just thinking."

There were people lying on the open lawn, leaning against trees and hiding behind the Eaglers' bushes. They whispered and kissed, their arms wrapped around each other. Even though I wouldn't have admitted it, watching those couples made me think of Wen and me, and how it wasn't meant to be.

nothing in the cry
of lovers suggests love is
just a fairy tale

I looked at Wen's sweet face and then back at the people in the shrubs.

"It doesn't remind me of anything," I said.

"You know what it reminds me of?" he whispered. "The secret beach. You know—the naked people? Don't you think so?"

"I guess," I said, not really meaning it.

He looked embarrassed and shrugged again. "It's just that they seemed so happy, like they were really in love. I hardly ever see people that happy together—not for long, anyway. Doesn't it make you think that maybe some people really do live happily ever after?"

It took a second for that to sink in, but when it did my eyes nearly swelled up and popped.

He'd noticed the same thing I had!

Obviously, maybe Wen and I were even more alike than I'd ever suspected. I'd never mentioned anything to anyone about the Mystery of the Old Naked People. Since I'd written about it only in my spiral notebook, Richard never posted it on the Web page. And yet, here was Wen talking about how lasting love was so rare—the same thoughts I'd been having ever since that night.

Standing so close, I suddenly felt again that he and I had some spiritual connection. If I was one with everything, then I was one with Wen.

"It's like a movie," I whispered. "A Zen romance."

We were standing very close and looking deep into each other's eyes, and I felt a sudden, strange electricity. An unexpected thrill ran up my legs when I realized we were getting even closer.

"Floey," he said, "I wanted to talk with you about what you wrote in your diary. About the deal between you and Azra. Don't I get any say?"

Everything around us dropped away. I felt like we were all alone. I gazed up at him and waited, unable to breathe. I closed my eyes, ready to lean toward him.

But then I caught myself.

This wasn't right. Azra and I had a *deal*. She was my best friend and she trusted me. Still, I could feel the Old Floey holding on for dear life, trying desperately not to be yanked out of this beautiful Zen moment. I had to get away from here, and right away.

That's when somebody touched my back.

"Wow, Floey!" Azra's voice said. "Leslie told me you made some changes, but I had no idea! Is it really you or am I talking to a very tall eggplant?"

I opened my eyes. Wen was studying my face.

"No, Azra," I managed. "It's just me."

• • •

Azra must have said more, but I wasn't really paying attention. I kept smiling, trying to act as normal as possible. I was glad I'd stayed loyal to our friendship, but I was frustrated, too. For a moment real love had seemed within reach, but once again it had been proven impossible after all.

After a few minutes, I felt I just had to leave. I told them I needed to go to the bathroom and then I bolted for the house.

I was so thirsty. There was a keg of beer in the kitchen, but after my bizarre champagne-induced performance at Lillian's wedding I didn't want to take any chances. Instead, I helped myself to the punch. I leaned back against the kitchen counter with a plastic cup full of the stuff and gulped it all down very quickly.

What was wrong with me? Where was my hard-earned emotional independence? I wanted to be extraordinary, but instead I'd discovered that I was just an extraordinary puddle of hormones.

I tried to pull myself together, but after a few minutes in the Eaglers' kitchen my head was spinning. I wondered vaguely if somebody had spiked the punch. I decided I should leave right away.

But then I thought, No. Don't panic. What would Lillian do?

"There you are," Dean Eagler said, his face close to my

ear. "I've been looking for you." I turned to him, but it was hard to focus with the room gently rocking around us. "Listen," he said, "you like music, right?"

I just stared at him.

"Come with me."

After the Wen incident, you might think there would have been a little voice in my head telling me to be cautious. *Another potential emotional disaster! Get away while you can!* Unfortunately, it turned out that deep down I was exactly like all the other girls I knew who would have given up two bust sizes if Dean Eagler would even glance in their general direction. This was definitely an un-wallpaper-like opportunity.

"Yes!" I said a little more enthusiastically than I meant to. "Yes, I'll come with you!"

• • •

I followed him to the back of the living room, where three ceiling-high bookshelves formed a private little nook. The stereo was on two of the shelves. As soon as we reached it, he turned the music down.

"Somebody keeps cranking it too high," he said. "It's so loud you can't really hear anything. I don't like that song anyway, do you?"

I shook my head. Actually, I hadn't even noticed the song.

There were rows and rows of alphabetically arranged CDs on five or six shelves. It reminded me of Wen's music collection, except it was much neater. Why did I always seem to be attracted to boys with enormous CD collections?

"You do like music, Floey. Right?"

"Sure. Yes." Uh-oh, my monosyllabic alter ego was rearing her ugly voice again.

He smiled. "What kind of music?"

I forced myself to say something intelligent. "I like all different kinds. New, old, pop, classical, punk, jazz, thrash, whatever. Surprise me." Right! That was more like it!

He scanned the shelves with his finger and reached for a CD on one of the middle rows. I was already feeling much better. I didn't need Wen. I had a tall, dark Elvis taking care of me.

"Here's something. Tell me what you think about this." He pulled it out, opened up the box and placed the CD in the slot. Before the music came on I noticed the cover—it was Mudslide Crush. Dean had chosen his own CD, the new one.

He put his arm around my shoulders. I hadn't expected that, but since he'd already lifted me right up into the air earlier in the evening, I decided it probably wasn't a big deal. The first song came on. It was one of my favorites, slow and moody and very, very cool, with a deep bass line that sounded like wading through a swamp.

"This is pretty good," I said casually. "Is it you?"

He flashed his killer smile. "Yeah. Glad you like it."

I nearly keeled over with happiness.

His hand slid down my back until it rested on my waist. That felt a little weird. Nice, but weird. I supposed he was just an affectionate guy. I wondered when I would get used to him standing next to me. He leaned in even closer. "I had a feeling you were into music," he said.

"You did?" I asked. "How come?"

"I can tell. I feel like I know you. You're an artist, like me."

"I am? What do you mean?"

"Oh, come on, Floey. The only difference between us is that I express myself through music while you express yourself with words." In the confusion of the moment, I wondered what he meant. I also wondered how long he was going to leave his hand on my waist. "This sleepy little town is no place for people like us. I can hardly breathe here."

I wasn't sure what to say. I just nodded.

"I'm so sick of all the average people crowding me with their average ideas, telling me what I can and can't do, man." I turned my head. His breath smelled of beer. He moved closer and spoke into my ear. "I know you know what I'm talking about, don't you? We're different from all the wallpaper people. We're in a class by ourselves."

Only then did I notice what he was wearing under the long plaid shirt that dangled below his waist. In the dark, I'd missed it.

Bike shorts.

That's when his hand slipped a little lower and I felt his fingers pressing firmly on my butt.

I suddenly felt like a fool.

Not long ago he hadn't shown the slightest interest in

my existence, and now here he was with his hand on my bum trying to convince me we were soul mates. Who knows, maybe he even believed it. He'd obviously read about me online and now he figured he knew all about me.

He stared into my eyes. Apparently, this was my cue to tell him I agreed with everything he was saying.

That's when I felt another hand, this one on my shoulder.

"We wondered where you went, Floey." It was Wen. "Everything okay?"

I was relieved Wen was here, but I didn't take my eyes off Dean. Suddenly he wasn't the young Elvis anymore; he was the old, fat Elvis—and I hated him. I gave him my angriest look, hoping it would deflate him.

"Yes," I said, suddenly the Frost Queen. "I'm just fine." I reached around and calmly lifted his hand off my waist and dropped it back to his side. "Dean was just telling me all about myself."

Dean's face changed. At first he looked confused, and then he shifted his weight and seemed almost angry, as if *I* were the one who'd insulted *him*.

"Are we, um, interrupting something?"

That's when I noticed Azra, Leslie and Kate behind Wen, gaping.

I was so angry I could have screamed, but I didn't want to make a big scene. Dean wasn't worth it. "No, you're not interrupting anything at all. I was just leaving." I stepped away from him, but before I got too far I had to turn back. "You have *no idea* who I am or how I feel!"

"Life is suffering, man," he said with a laugh. "Zen you die."

I turned away again and pushed past my surprised friends, but that's when I knocked right into somebody else. It was Miss Halter Top.

Her drink spilled to the floor. When she recovered and looked up to see who had done this, I wondered for a moment if, when she recognized me, she would really try to fight me this time. Instead, she just narrowed her eyes.

"Oh," she said. "It's *you*."

I scrambled away from her. Thankfully, she didn't try to follow me. All I wanted was to get away from this place, away from Dean. Now I knew the truth: Dean wasn't like Elvis at all—he was just some conceited guy I never wanted to see again. But before I could escape, another wall of people blocked my path.

That's when Azra, Wen and Leslie caught up with me a second time. All three of them looked worried, even a little angry.

"Did he do anything to you?" Azra asked.

"No," I managed. "I'm fine."

"Because if he did . . ."

But I didn't wait to hear. I just wanted to leave.

"Just get me out of here."

chapterthirteen:

life is suffering

• • • • • • • • • • • •

Monday, July 21, 9:30 a.m.

Dear F,

My head hurts.

It's going to be another gross, muggy day—I can already feel it. Ma is out whacking a ball around with Gary. Richard and Tish are outside, God only knows where. I'm sitting in bed eating a bowl of cereal. Frank Sinatra is resting against my leg. I'm surprised he'd sit this close. Maybe he misses me. Or maybe he's just slumming it.

Oh, great, now he's cleaning himself.

While I eat my soggy, tasteless breakfast and the ferret licks his private parts, I'll just take this moment to consider the sorry state of my life. The past three and a half weeks kind of all blur together in my head. My boyfriend dumped me and didn't know it, evil children invaded my home, a strange network of eleven-year-old boys put my private thoughts on the Internet and sold an embarrassing picture of me to strangers and last night (was that really only last night?) I was groped by a Neanderthal bass player. Worst of all, I nearly betrayed my very best friend.

I guess that about sums it up.

At least I have a pen pal who sends me poetry. That's kind of nice.

Wait. On second thought, if Dean knows about the Web site, then it's not just little boys reading it anymore. Calvin's inspiration was probably his computer monitor, just like Dean's was.

Chalk up another one for the extraordinary, always fascinating New Floey Packer.

One thing was sure: I had to do something about floeysprivatelife.com.

I just wasn't sure what yet.

When I came out of my room, there was a note from Ma telling me to do the laundry. Richard had made his bed again—the first time in a few days. After I sleepwalked through the bedrooms, I checked the dirty laundry hamper.

I imagined what Lillian and Helmut were doing at that exact moment: probably relaxing hand in hand under some picture-perfect palm tree. This was the last week of their honeymoon. Friday night they'd arrive back home, and then on Monday they'd move to New York to start their new glamorous lives. After that they'd live happily ever after.

No, wait. That probably wasn't true.

love and happiness
happily ever after
blah blah blah blah blah

The hamper was full, so I heaved it down to the basement and tipped everything onto the floor in front of the washing machine. Mixed in with everything else were the sheets I'd put on Richard's bed only the day before. He must have made his bed with new clean sheets and then thrown the old ones in the hamper. That was strange.

Why would he need to wash his sheets so soon?

But then I noticed that one of the sheets had a big dark circle in the middle.

It was wet, and it had the unmistakable smell of pee.

That's when the door creaked behind me. I jumped.

After I spun around, the door opened very slowly and Tish gradually appeared. Actually, it wasn't all of Tish, exactly. Just her head.

"Floey?"

"What is it, Tish? You scared me!"

She peered cautiously around the door. She didn't say anything. She just looked at me. After a moment I got pretty frustrated with her.

"Come on, what is it?"

"You have to come with me," she said finally. "We'd better hurry. They might come back."

"Who?"

But she didn't answer. I followed her up the stairs and into the little office. She switched on the computer.

"Tell me what's going on."

"Billy has a new idea," she whispered. "He organized a bunch of his friends to carry cameras, digital ones if they have them, to take pictures."

"Pictures? Of what?"

The computer came up, and she opened the browser. "I have to show you. Richard gave me his password." She kept typing and clicking until finally she opened an e-mail message that had a bunch of attached images.

"It's one of these." She double-clicked on the first one.

A photograph popped up on the screen. The image was pretty fuzzy, but I knew what it was. It was a picture of me, apparently taken from across Dean's driveway. I was standing at Dean's front door.

"That's horrible!" I said. "You mean to tell me they had somebody waiting for me in Dean Eagler's yard?"

"They're going to start putting these up as soon as Richard sets up the new page. That's not the one I was looking for. They sent so many. Everybody's excited about it."

This was starting to get really scary.

She opened up a bunch of different pictures, one at a time. One showed me hiding my bike under a bush. Another showed me in Dean's backyard talking to Leslie and Kate. I was barely visible in the dim light.

"This must be it," she said finally. She glanced nervously at me before she tapped the mouse.

The screen filled with the image of two people standing next to a tree. It wasn't a great shot. Whoever had taken it might have been twenty feet or so away, and shadows from the floodlights made it hard to make out the details. A boy and girl stood very close together. In fact, the girl leaned back against the tree while the boy leaned against her. It was one of the couples making out in Dean's backyard. At first I didn't understand, but then I noticed the girl's short straight dark hair. I knew it well.

"Hey, that's Azra!" I said. I'd told Azra to stay at the party, that I wanted to come home alone. "Wow. Who's the guy?"

Tish looked at me uneasily, so I stared at the picture again. I couldn't see his whole face, but he had longish blond hair and a Hawaiian shirt. And black-framed plastic glasses.

All of a sudden I couldn't breathe.

"I thought this might be a big deal to you," she said. "I wasn't sure I should show you, but I figured you'd see it after Billy makes Richard write the code. I didn't want you to find out like that. They're working this into a special new page. I wanted you to know before it goes up."

Now I understood. Azra said that she'd forgiven me about what I'd written in the diary. That we were still friends. That our deal about Wen was the same as ever.

But Azra was a big faker. Everything she'd said was an act.

I didn't know which made me feel worst: that the one boy I really liked had chosen somebody else, that the somebody else was Azra or that my best friend had betrayed me.

"Was I wrong to show you? Are you mad at me?"

But I couldn't say anything just then. My throat was tightening up. I didn't want to cry in front of her, so I left the room as fast as I could.

"Where are you going?" she called.

I didn't answer. I raced outside to get my bicycle.

On the steps, I ran into Billy with Richard right behind him. Billy stopped and stared. "What the hell happened to your hair?"

I considered screaming at them, but I stopped myself. I could do better than that, I just needed to think of a way. Plus, I had something else to take care of first.

I leapt past them, grabbed my bike from under the stairs. In the warm, heavy air, I pumped and sweated my way down the street, past the cemetery and up and down the hilly road into town, toward the YMCA.

• • •

Gray clouds cluttered the sky. By the time I pulled into the YMCA lot the air felt even thicker, like it was about to rain. In the open field behind the chain-link fence, little kids ran around stuffing balls, bats and bases into burlap sacks, dragging them toward the main building.

There she was. She was carrying one of the bigger sacks.

I didn't have time to bike around the fence. The day-campers were moving toward the door so fast that I thought she might get inside before I reached her. That's why I stopped at the metal chain links, grabbed them and started shouting her name.

"Azraaa! Azraaaa!"

The kids turned to look. Azra waved, then dropped her bag by the brick wall and trotted over to me. She looked as hot as I felt.

"Hey, Floey. What are you doing here? You never came by to see me before." She sounded friendly, but I could hear something uneasy in her voice. Through the fence that separated us, a wire diamond framed her smiling face. She tilted her head. "What's the sound of one hand clapping?"

"I know about you and Wen," I said.

Her smile faded. I can't be sure if it was guilt that flashed into her eyes, but whatever it was, it didn't last long. All of a sudden, to my complete and utter surprise, she burst into tears.

"Oh, Floey!" she bawled, running up closer to me but covering her face with her hands. "I don't know what to do!"

I could only stare. I wasn't sure what to think.

"It wasn't me," she said from the other side of the fence. "Wen told me he read about our deal and was hurt that we didn't even consider whether he had feelings about it. And the next thing I knew, he . . . he kissed me!"

I could hardly believe my ears. "He did? And you tried to stop him?"

She shook her head. "I was too surprised! He told me

he's liked me for a long time. He said he didn't want to hurt *you,* though. He even said he tried to talk to you about it last night, but I guess I interrupted him. And then he felt uncomfortable."

All at once, I couldn't speak. I felt like I'd been punched in the stomach, like all the air had been knocked out of me.

"What could I do, Floey?" she asked, wiping the tears from her face. "You know how much I've always liked him. Last night was wonderful and horrible at the same time. I couldn't sleep. I'm so confused! I want to be with Wen, but I don't want to lose my best friend!"

For a moment, even with the storm rising inside me, I felt sorry for her. A part of me wanted somehow to reach through the fence and hold her hand and tell her it was okay.

But I couldn't.

"We had an agreement," I said finally. "And you threw it away."

"But . . . but he came to me, not the other way around."

I pretended not to hear her. "And you're supposed to be my friend?"

She stared at me. "I was hoping you'd understand."

"Oh, I understand, all right. I understand completely. It was between the two of us, and you decided to toss me aside."

She looked hurt. "No. That wasn't it at all."

I let go of the fence, spun my bike around and pushed it a few feet closer to the road. I knew that what I was doing was mean, but I couldn't stop myself.

I turned back to face her. "So much for trust."

Her mouth dropped. "What?" A moment later her expression hardened and she stepped right up to the fence. She looked ready for a fight. "What do you know about trust? From what I read, it didn't seem like *you* thought we even *had* an agreement."

It was my turn to be surprised and hurt.

I didn't know what to say. "Didn't you already forgive me for that?" I asked, realizing for the first time what a terrible thing I was doing. "You said you believed those were just stupid ideas I wrote down, remember? They didn't mean anything?"

She shrugged and her red eyes narrowed. "It isn't my fault that Wen likes me and not you. Besides, after seeing you with Dean Eagler last night, I didn't think it'd matter to you."

That was low, but I ignored her. "So . . . ," I began, trying to regain control of the conversation. "So you decided to ditch me just like that? What happened to the Three Blind Mice?"

"I guess we never really knew the real Floey, did we? Maybe we really *were* blind." She wiped her eyes and took a couple of steps backward toward the building. "Listen, Miss Dazzling and Charming. I have to go back."

That was it. I was too hurt to stop now. When she turned and started walking away I ran back to the fence and shouted through the links. "I can't believe you, Azra! I guess the minute a person stands out a little from her old crowd, that's when jealousy comes out, isn't it? That's when she finds out who her friends really are! How could you do this to me? Traitor!"

She turned around. "Yeah? Well, you did it to me first. Maybe when you're really famous you can have a whole new set of friends."

"Maybe you're right! You ought to know about new friends! Now that you and Leslie are so tight, I guess it's out with the old and in with the new!"

"Huh?" She squinted and crossed her arms on her chest. "I guess you don't realize it, but Leslie's a great person and *she* really likes *you*. But you know what? *I* don't like the new, fabulous, famous Floey Packer, okay? I preferred my old, invisible, ordinary friend. I miss her."

"There's nothing wrong with the new me. And having an audience can bring out the best in a person."

She stared at me and shook her head. "Who *are* you?" After a moment she turned back again.

"Don't walk away from me!" I called. "We're not done!"

"Yes, we are," she said.

After that, I couldn't make her come back, no matter what I shouted through the chain links.

• • •

In the moments before the storm, there was nobody on the roads. Nobody to see me fly by, nobody walking around town, no kids playing in any of the front yards.

I had an eerie feeling I was the last person on earth.

How could I have thought Wen was interested in me when all along it was Azra? How could I have made such a mistake? And why didn't he like me? And how could they have done this to me?

Back in front of my house I could see Richard and Tish watching TV through our big front window. I couldn't bring myself to go back into the house, so I turned around and headed back in the direction I'd come from.

puke garbage hateful
stinking rotten doom vomit
dead dark cold awful

Past the park at the end of my road, the air was so thick and hot it felt like I was biking through soup. I turned left in the direction of the secret beach. But that made me think of the Old Naked People. Which made me think of Wen. Which made me even more miserable.

I tried to clear my mind. I needed to force Wen and Azra out of my head. Lillian would be home soon. Aunt Sarah too.

Finally I'd be free of my awful cousins. Thank God.

A raindrop fell on my neck. The clouds hung darker now. This could be the start of a quick summer shower or a big storm. I figured if I pedaled fast I'd probably make it to Gary's studio before it really started pouring.

I pumped harder.

By the time I'd pedaled up the big hill, the sweat dripped down my forehead into my eyes. Fatter raindrops fell all around me, soaking into my shirt and cooling me a little. I was close to the turnoff for the secret beach now, about halfway back to town, so I didn't turn around.

Through the trees I could see the old cottage. I considered turning down the path. Maybe if I talked with the old people I'd feel better. Should I walk right up to their door and knock?

No. That was crazy.

Besides, there was no car in the driveway. They were probably renters and long gone now.

And anyway, Wen and I were probably *both* wrong about the Old Naked People. What we saw couldn't have been real love. And even if it was, it had to be a fluke. In either case, who cared? After Calvin and Dean and Wen, I never wanted anything else to do with those kinds of crazy ideas. It was just one disappointment after another. And then there was Azra. But I didn't really *need* friends anymore, did I? I was famous now, sort of. Even if it was a solitary life, wouldn't the Floey of the future choose an extraordinary life over an ordinary one misspent chasing the impossible?

Yes. She would. Definitely.

Suddenly, the rain hammered down. It completely soaked my hair and made my clothes heavy. Water dripped into my face, but I didn't care. Rain doesn't matter when you can't get any wetter.

Or when you don't care about anything anymore.

Just then I heard a loud *whoosh*, like a tidal wave crashing over me. I hadn't noticed the huge puddle at the bottom of the hill I'd been racing down. A lake of water flew up at me, and suddenly my bike and I were sliding across the sidewalk. But in my mind it was as if the water had come from some other place, floating slowly through the air and drenching me like a gradually rising flood. And then, for a moment, I was at our back door again, standing in the pouring rain, locked out of Lillian's wedding reception.

I was obviously having another Pivotal Life Moment. A Zen crisis.

In impossibly slow motion, I reached out to break my fall.

Life is suffering, Zen you die.

What I remember is that just after I hit the ground and just before I felt the scraping pain in my palms and knees, I imagined I heard a stranger calling my name.

". . . FLOEEEEEY!"

I pictured a crowd of grinning faces staring at me through their cameras. I screamed and crashed onto the sidewalk. Falling and sliding across the pavement couldn't have taken more than a second or two, but it felt like that moment went on and on.

I stayed in a heap for a while, not because I couldn't get up but because I didn't want to. When I finally pulled myself off the sidewalk, the world still hadn't sped back up to normal speed. I held my hands in front of my face. My palms were scraped and bleeding and my leg stung. Rain poured all over me, gushing down my hair and nose and back. And even though I could feel the pain in my hands, it was like I really wasn't feeling it at all. I was me, but I was also someone outside of me, someone separate, just watching.

I sat on the sidewalk next to my bike for a long time, letting the rain clean the blood from my skin. Lines of violet, runoff from the dye, washed across the sidewalk. I stared through the woods toward the cove. In a moment of clarity I realized that my crazy new life couldn't continue like this.

Everything had to stop.

Something else had to start.

All at once I knew exactly what I was going to do.

chapter fourteen:

in which i'm so mad that

i pant like a wild animal

The rain had stopped. Tish sat on the front step staring at me like I was nuts. I must have looked nuts. I was still dripping wet, out of breath and mad mad mad.

"Where's Richard?" I demanded.

"On the phone," she said. And then she whispered, "With Billy."

I stormed into the house, my feet squelching.

"Richard! Richard!"

He was standing by the wall, holding the phone to his ear and wrapping the cord nervously around his finger. One look at me and his face turned even paler than usual.

"It's Floey. I'll have to call you back," he said. "Yes, I *promise*. I'll call *right back*." He put the receiver on its hook and shrank against the wall, waiting for me.

"I know everything," I said, still catching my breath.

"Everything?" he said. There wasn't an ounce of guilt in his voice. He was obviously trying to sound innocent. "What about?"

"Don't try that with me, you little monster! The spy

club, the Web site—you know exactly what. You better pull the plug right this minute if you know what's good for you!"

From his expression, it seemed like he might keep trying to deny it, but after a moment his face changed. He sidestepped toward the hallway.

Then he ran.

"You little horror!" I shouted. I chased him. He was down the hall in no time, so I followed him out the back door and into the field behind our house. For a little runt he ran pretty fast. He'd already reached the tall grass when I caught up with him and pulled him down.

"*Aaah!* Get off me!"

"I'm not playing any more stupid games with you." I spun him around and sat on his chest. "You better put a stop to it. If you think everything's just going to continue the same until you go home, you're wrong!"

He struggled but I weighed too much for him. "I can't! It's not me you want, it's Billy!"

This wasn't going to be easy. I didn't know how to shut the Web site down myself, so he had to do it. But how was I supposed to *make* him?

Then I remembered cleaning his room. I suddenly saw myself back in the basement, sorting the laundry, seeing his sheets.

His sheets.

He squirmed but I had him pinned. He looked really scared.

"I know something about you that you don't want anyone

to find out," I said through my teeth. "Unless you pull down that Web site, I'll tell everyone. And I mean *everyone*."

He stopped struggling and stared at me. "What do you know?"

"You mean apart from the fact that you're a little weasel?" He didn't reply. I put my face closer to his. Water from my hair dripped onto his forehead. I let him wait.

"What is it? What?"

"You're a bed wetter, aren't you, Richard?"

His eyes grew wide. I had him.

"Dear Future Floey," I said. "Why are Richard's sheets wet every other morning? Does his mommy know he still has trouble controlling his bladder at night? Eleven years old. Pretty embarrassing."

His lips started to quiver.

"How about if, instead of putting that in my diary, I just hand it right to Billy? And while I'm at it, how about if I send it to your little friends in Chicago, too? If you have any. There are a lot of e-mail addresses on that message board. Do any of those readers go to your school? I bet somebody does."

His eyes grew even wider, and then he started to cry. By then Tish had appeared at the edge of the tall grass. She looked frightened too.

"Don't do it!" he begged. "Please!"

"After what you've done to me, why shouldn't I?"

"Don't tell anybody at home! You don't know what they'll say. It'd be . . . awful!"

"Oh, stop crying, you baby," I said. "You should have

thought of that before you did such terrible things. How could you?" But he kept crying. It went on and on. After a while, I actually felt embarrassed for him. "And how about your mother? What'll she say when she finds out what you've been up to?"

"Don't get me in trouble!" he pleaded, still weeping and sniveling. "Please don't tell!"

He was so pitiful I had to shake my head. "Pull down the Web site right now and I'll think about it."

"I can't," he sobbed. "It's too important now!"

"Too important? What are you talking about?"

"To Billy and those kids, it's a really huge game. The biggest."

"It's true," Tish said. "Those guys think the spy club is the coolest extracurricular activity ever invented."

"And it's all Billy's. You don't know how furious he'd be if I took it down."

"What do you mean Billy'd be furious?" I said. "What do I care what he thinks? And it's not his site, it's *yours*—so turn it off!"

He thrashed around under me, making the tall, wet grass whip and rustle around our heads. "You don't get it! Sure, it's my site. I mean, I put it up, but really it's always been Billy's. He's the one in charge. And now there's a whole crowd of kids, and he's the leader. If I pull it down, he won't let me get away with it. But I never put up your last name or address or anything anybody could use to identify you. Did you even notice that?"

I peered into his eyes and tried to understand. I still

didn't see why Billy mattered so much to him. He wasn't making sense.

All of a sudden, he stopped struggling. "I never wanted it to go this far, I really didn't. But Billy kept making the whole thing bigger and bigger. He wouldn't let it drop."

"So why are you friends with him?"

He didn't answer right away. He looked at Tish and took a couple of long breaths, and then he closed his eyes. "He was the only cool guy I've ever been friends with, Floey. At home, kids make fun of me. They give me wedgies and call me names. He didn't. He made me his buddy." He opened his eyes. "After a few days, he wasn't my buddy anymore, but by then it was too late."

"That's no excuse! You should have stood up to him, Richard. What's the matter with you?"

He looked at me like I was insane. "I'm scared of him, Floey. I'm terrified. Everybody is." All of a sudden, fresh tears dribbled into his already wet hair.

That's when, believe it or not, I actually started to feel sorry for him. When I looked in his eyes I could tell he wasn't kidding. The boy was petrified. Was all this just because Richard was doing the same thing I was doing—trying to be fabulous?

Tish stood perfectly still in the grass, watching us from a safe distance.

"All right, calm down," I said, getting off him. But he still lay there, bawling like a newborn. "Get a grip on yourself, will you? Let's think this through. What if I can come up with a way for us to put a stop to this crazy stuff, all of it, and get even with Billy, too—all without him knowing you had anything to do with it. Will you help me?"

What came out of Richard's mouth next was only a quiet moan, a whimper, barely loud enough to hear. But then he tried again. "He'll beat me up. You have no idea how mean he can get."

"Maybe," I said. "But you'll be going home soon. If I tell your friends in Chicago about your little problem, what will happen when you get home?"

Richard sighed. "If I help, Billy won't know *and* you won't tell my mom about this *and* you won't tell anybody about the . . . you know, the bed?"

"All right. If you'll help me, I won't tell. But it'll cost you."

He took another long breath and closed his eyes.

Slowly, the worried look on Tish's face changed to a smile.

chapter fifteen:

in which

i am exposed

• • • • • • • • • • • •

At exactly 11:20 that night, I slipped out of bed and nudged Tish to get up. She was still awake. She had already picked out her darkest clothes and was wearing them in bed. A moment later we climbed out the window and onto the grass. Richard was leaning against the house waiting for us, just as I'd told him to. He looked worried.

"Did you bring the firecrackers?" I whispered.

He nodded. He handed me a little box.

In the glow from Richard's flashlight, Tish looked jittery and excited. "Do you have the camera?" she whispered louder than I thought was safe.

I nodded and led them farther away from the house and into the field.

That afternoon Gary had let me borrow one of his digital camcorders and some other equipment. But Tish and I had never used a camcorder, so we weren't sure how it worked. Since Gary had given me a couple of disks, we decided to use one of them for practice. We practiced on Frank Sinatra. As soon as the camera was on him, he hopped down from the bookshelf to the floor. I don't think he liked to be recorded. We followed him as he stalked through the kitchen and into the bathroom. He went straight to his litter box and did a big turd. I think he did it on purpose.

Just to spite him, I kept filming anyway.

Now, in the darkness of my yard, I pulled Gary's camcorder from my backpack and handed it to Tish. "And you're *sure* everybody's coming?"

"Yes," Richard said anxiously. "They'll all be there."

"Well, you'd better go meet them, then. Go on, hurry. You don't want anybody to suspect anything, do you?"

He gave me one last frightened look and set off across the lawn and down the street. We waited five minutes before following him, staying in the shadows as much as possible.

My plan was simple: we'd lure Billy and all his friends together and then we'd ambush them—all on camera. Since Richard would be with them the whole time, they'd have no idea he'd helped us.

That afternoon I'd made him publish a new entry on the Web site. It was short:

<u>Monday, July 21, 2:00 p.m.</u>

Dear Floey of Tomorrow,

I feel wild and free and especially at one with the universe today. I want to do something extraordinary, something I've never done before. At *midnight, under the summer moon over Otis Cove, I'll dance naked like my ancient ancestors. Liberated from the material demands of clothing, my inner primitive spirit will connect openly with the spirits of the mystical future. I will howl at the moon and swim in the water, as naked as the day I was born, as free as I was meant to be.*

I figured that ought to do the trick.

"Keep your head down," I said, pulling Tish out of the light as two boys on bicycles came up the street. We stood still and let them pass. I couldn't hear what they whispered, but they were laughing and heading toward the cove.

Even with the slowdown, Tish and I made pretty good time. When we reached the path we put away our flashlights and started into the trees. I squeezed the button to light up my watch. It was 11:53.

In the woods we had to keep very quiet. Earlier that day I'd shown Richard the secret beach (after tonight, it wouldn't be so secret anymore) and pointed out exactly where I wanted him to bring the little creeps. It had been days since I'd seen a car in the driveway of the cottage, so I was confident that the beach would be all mine tonight. I'd told Richard to lead the spy club boys from the opposite direction, but there was still a chance Tish and I might run into one of them. Inside the cover of the trees it was especially dark. Without our flashlights, we had to move slowly and wave our hands in front of us so we wouldn't walk into a tree or a branch.

We crept through the tall grass toward the little clearing. Well before we came to the place where Wen, Azra and I had sat on the Fourth of July, we stopped and crouched down.

I checked my watch again: 11:57.

The cove looked beautiful. Moonlight glittered across the water and reflected on the boats moored on the other side. It was a much brighter night than the last time I had been here, and when I raised my head a little I could see into the clearing pretty well. Other than the gentle sounds of the waves and the crickets, everything was quiet. I tried to settle in, but I wasn't very comfortable crouching. A long moment passed, and I still didn't hear anything or anybody. I worried that something was wrong.

Tish put her mouth to my ear. "Where is everyone?"

"I don't know," I whispered back.

We crouched for another couple of minutes, careful not to move or make a sound. With only a minute to go until midnight, I was worried that my plan had gone wrong, that the boys knew I knew about them and had stayed home. But just then, a few yards ahead of us and to our left, I heard somebody whisper. After that, ahead of us but more to our right, somebody else said "Shhh!" The whispering stopped, but the grass rustled a little. That made me feel better. At least I knew Tish and I weren't the only people hiding in the reeds. I was glad we'd been careful to sit far enough back from where we'd told Richard to bring the spy club.

I checked my watch again. Midnight.

"Where is she?" somebody said.

"Aww, she's not going to show," whispered somebody else.

We'd been squatting as still as we could. My knees hurt. I don't know whether it was the heat or that I was so nervous, but I was sweating pretty hard. Waiting had been excruciating.

Tish put her mouth to my ear again. "Ready?"

I nodded and reached into my pocket.

But then, unexpectedly, I heard the sound of somebody humming. It was a woman, and it was coming from the direction of the old cottage. What was this? How could anyone have been staying there? There'd been no lights and no car in the driveway. This would ruin everything!

Tish elbowed me.

I froze, a lighter and Richard's box of firecrackers ready in my hands.

The whispering that had been building in our little area behind the clearing suddenly went silent. Carefully, I peered over the grass to see who was coming. The cottage porch light was on now. In silhouette, I could also make out the tops of a few heads that had risen just high enough to see over the reeds. Judging by the number of shadowy figures peering from the grass, it seemed like there might be more kids hiding with us than I'd imagined there would be. Were there ten, twelve? I couldn't be sure.

My heart was beating even faster now. I wasn't sure what to do. I put the firecrackers back in my pocket.

The humming was high and pretty, and it was directly in

front of us now. The woman had a flashlight, and the glow made the individual reeds stand out tall and dark. The wall of grass rustled and finally opened up. The silhouetted heads dropped back out of sight. The lady who stepped out looked like she was carrying a towel. Who was she? In the darkness, I wondered if the monsters thought they were looking at me.

And then I recognized the short hair. That's when I realized with sudden horror who had come back to the beach.

The Old Naked People.

Immediately behind the woman, two other people stepped into view: first the skinny lady with the long white hair, and behind her the bald man with the big gut. By now it must have been pretty obvious to the boys that none of these people was me because the flashlight had given us a quick glimpse of them.

And just like the other night, they were, as Lillian would say, au naturel. Entirely and utterly buck.

I stopped breathing. How could this have happened? Had they parked somewhere new, maybe on the far side of the house? Whatever it was, I'd made a terrible mistake. I'd felt bad enough stumbling onto them the first time, but now I'd brought an even bigger audience. This was a nightmare!

Somebody to my right gasped. The nearby grass moved just a little. But the old people didn't seem to notice. "Yes, it *is* a little better down here," the long-haired lady said. "Not so oppressive."

"Well, I'm sure as hell not waiting for anybody," the old

man said. He moved past them and ran into the cool water. The women followed him, first wading in and then sitting down in the water up to their necks.

I wondered vaguely where the other man was. The bear. Not that it really mattered. So far my plan had completely backfired, and there was only one sensible thing to do, which is what Tish suggested right then:

"Oh my God, Floey," she said, wide-eyed, yanking at my arm. "We better run!"

And I almost did, too. I almost bolted back into the woods, hoping to fade unnoticed into the scenery like so many times before. But something held me back. A moment later I realized what it was: anger. I couldn't let it end like this. The spy club boys were supposed to be the ones running away, not me. Of course, if I could have somehow changed things so that the Old Naked People weren't involved, I certainly would have. But now it was too late. Their late-night skinny-dipping ritual, if that was what it was, had already been violated. The least I could do was let them know.

I put my hand on Tish's arm to keep her from running, and then I pulled out Richard's box again. Inside were a couple of little red tubes and a gray sphere about the size of a golf ball. I picked out one of the tubes.

"Floey, what are you *doing*?"

From my other pocket I pulled out the lighter.

"Get the camera ready," I whispered.

Her eyes darted from me to the beach and back again. She looked uncertain, but she raised Gary's camcorder and turned it on. I found the string on the little tube, and keeping it low to hide the flame, I flipped the lighter and lit the fuse. Then I threw it as hard as I could. The firecracker landed in the middle of the clearing, hissing and spitting.

From the water, the man said, "What the hell is that?"

After a few seconds a bright green line shot into the air and burst over our heads in a brilliant umbrella of color, the embers floating down over the water.

As I lit the second tube, one of the women called out, "Tom, there's somebody here!"

The second one landed pretty near the first. After a few hisses and sparks it shot up even higher. By the time it burst into a fluorescent pink ball, I'd tossed the last firecracker, the gray sphere, which banged and cracked like gunfire.

That's when all hell broke loose.

The short-haired lady screamed. The man with the gut, the one they'd called Tom, lunged toward the beach just as I switched on Gary's portable spotlight, which I'd pulled from my backpack. The reeds sprang to life, suddenly shaking and moving like a big, frightened animal that had been rudely woken up. Terrified boys appeared from the grass, scrambling to their feet, pure panic on their faces. There were more of them than I'd imagined, twenty or so, maybe more. I tried to move the light around so Tish's camera could catch each of them.

Just at that moment, the reeds across the clearing opened up and the missing man stepped out, bigger and broader-shouldered than I'd remembered, and very, very angry.

"There they are!" shouted the huge naked man. "Come out here, you little bastards!"

Tom and the giant man reached the reeds at about the same time. That's when the spy club really started screaming. Everything happened in a matter of seconds. I held up the spotlight, doing my best to shine it on the boys and not the naked people. The men fought and slashed their way through the tall grass toward us, first chasing after the nearest boys, the ones sitting at the front. I knew it wouldn't be long before the two enraged men would get close enough to Tish and me and we'd have to hightail it out of there. The whole place was complete chaos. It was as if two furious grizzlies had come growling into the clearing. The petrified boys could hardly scramble away fast enough. Shouting and crying, some of them ran into and over each other to get back to the main beach or into the woods.

• • •

Tish and I escaped the same way we'd come in. Once we reached the road, we ran down the hill and past the cemetery. A couple of boys on bikes shot past us, huffing and puffing. When we reached the park at the end of my street we felt safe, so we stopped. I set the heavy backpack down in front of a bush. I needed to catch my breath.

"Did you see their faces!" gasped Tish, dropping down

to the ground. "I don't know if I'll ever have that much fun again as long as I live!"

"I saw them," I said. I was still breathing pretty heavily, so I rested against a tree. I hoped all this wouldn't discourage the Old Naked People from ever skinny-dipping hand in hand again.

That would be a tragedy.

Tish leaned back on her elbows. "Just wait until tomorrow when those guys go onto the Internet to look for your diary but they see themselves instead!" She laughed so hard that tears streamed down her face.

All of a sudden, we heard a scream from down the street.

It sounded like Richard's voice.

Tish grabbed the backpack and we crept back to the edge of the road to see if we could make out what was happening in the darkness. Around the corner, across the street from the cemetery, were a nursery school and a church. At the other end of the school parking lot there were four or five shadows holding flashlights.

And in the middle of the circle of flashlights stood Richard.

chapter sixteen:

in which my cousin takes a punch

• • • • • • • • • • • •

Billy grabbed Richard by the arm. Richard struggled, but with the big gorilla holding him and the other boys all around him there wasn't much point.

"Hilarious," Billy said in that high voice of his. "You think you're pretty funny, Richard, don't you?"

Richard looked terrified. He didn't speak.

"Let him go, Billy!" I called. "It was *my* idea, not his. He didn't know anything about it."

With his free hand, Billy took out his flashlight and shined it on my face. The other boys did the same. For a moment, I couldn't see anything.

"Sure he didn't," Billy called back. And then, dragging Richard along, he started walking toward me. "Where's that camera, Floey? Hand it over."

In this strange, scary moment, with Billy coming for me, a crowd of angry eleven-year-olds staring at me from the shadows and blinding bright lights shining directly in my face, I realized that in a bizarre way, I'd gotten what I thought I wanted. Everyone was looking at me. A lot of people knew who I was. In a way, the New Floey was a big success. Only, I didn't want what she wanted anymore. All I wanted was for everyone to leave Richard alone. To leave *me* alone. I wanted to fade away to nothing.

I wanted to be the wallpaper again.

I didn't move. "Why did you watch me from your window, Billy?" I called out finally. "What's the matter with you? Why did you tell your stupid spy club to follow me around? Why won't you leave me alone?"

"You should know," he said, still coming. The other shadow-boys were right behind him. "After all, like you say, we're not separate. It's all Zen!" He laughed. "If I'm so connected to you and you to me, why do you have to ask? One hand clapping, right?"

"Why don't you answer me? You *know* that doesn't make any sense!"

"Isn't it obvious?" Tish asked from behind me. "He *likes* you, Floey."

If she hadn't turned her flashlight onto Billy's face, I probably wouldn't have seen it turn red. It glowed like a ripe tomato.

"Problem is," Tish continued, "this is all you can think of to get Floey's attention, isn't it, Billy? You're too stupid and insecure to try anything else. Right, Billy?"

His big gorilla mouth tightened.

I didn't know whether to laugh or scream.

"Get that light off me!" he said, walking faster. He was

in the middle of the street and only a few cemetery rows away. He pointed his flashlight back at Tish. "And shut your mouth, Chunky Monkey!"

But that's when Richard bit down on Billy's hand.

Hard.

Billy stopped. His scream sounded like a little girl's. "*Ooowwooowwww!*"

Out of his grasp, Richard tried to run. Unfortunately, he didn't get farther than the grass at the edge of the sidewalk before the other boys grabbed him and dragged him back. I didn't know whether to be mad at him for being so stupid or proud of him for finally standing up to Billy.

"Keep him down!" one of the boys said. Some of the others pushed Richard and held his face to the ground.

"I'm bleeding!" Billy shouted. "I think he bit right through to the bone!"

He put his knuckle in his mouth and sucked on it. After a moment, he walked up to Richard, flexing his fingers. "That was stupid. You didn't think I was just going to let you get away with that, did you?" And then to his friends he said, "Stand him up."

Tish screamed.

"No!" I shouted.

But Billy swung his fist back and belted Richard a good one, right in the stomach. Richard gasped and fell back to his knees.

"Leave him alone!" I shouted. "He's half your size!"

Billy turned back to me and smiled. "No. Not till I get that camera."

"Okay, okay!" I said. "Leave him alone and I'll give you the disk!"

Billy considered my offer and nodded. "All right, Fabulous Floey of the Future. Deal. Give me the disk and I'll let him go."

But that's when Richard finally said something. At first I wasn't sure it was him, but it was. "Don't do it, Floey," he said.

Billy turned and glared at him. I thought he might hit him again.

"I don't want you to," Richard continued, trying to pull himself up. "Let him beat me up, I don't care. Don't let him have the disk."

I stared at him. After the way he'd cried that afternoon, I didn't think he had it in him. Still, I wasn't going to let Billy beat him up.

"The disk isn't that important, Richard."

Tish had the backpack, and she beat me to it. She unzipped it, pulled out what she needed and left the bag near me while she walked across the street to Billy. "Here," she said, glaring at him. "Take it. Now let him go."

He examined the little piece of plastic with his flashlight. "Good," he said. "This is good."

A moment later, he and the other shadowy boys from the spy club were running away down the street, shouting and laughing in the darkness.

And then they were gone.

• • •

I went over to Richard. "Are you okay?"

"I'm fine," he said, waving me off him. "He just winded me for a second, that's all." He didn't look fine. In fact, he looked like he might wet his pants. He stood up and brushed himself off. "I can't believe you guys just did that for me."

"I can't either," Tish said. "You didn't deserve it."

For a while, the only sound was from the crickets. I wondered if we really were alone now. The spy club had come and gone so quickly. But eventually I picked up the backpack and we walked home. None of us said another word.

Naturally, I was disappointed with the evening. True, since the boys knew I was on to them, the Web site was finished. But now that they had the disk, I felt like they'd gotten away with something. I'd wanted those embarrassing images of terrified spy club boys to be the final pictures on the Web site, their grand farewell. It only seemed fair.

As soon as we got to my backyard again, just before I turned off my flashlight, I heard Tish giggle.

"What are you laughing about?" I whispered.

"I have a secret," she whispered back. She came closer so that even if there was somebody else listening, only Richard and I would hear.

We leaned in close.

"I switched the disks."

She pulled a disk out of her pants pocket and held it up to us. Richard and I stared at it, still not sure what she meant.

"*This* is the one from the beach," she said.

"So . . . ," I said, just beginning to understand, "does that mean Billy has . . ."

She nodded and giggled again.

"They have the one of Frank Sinatra."

I imagined Billy and his friends standing around a television. Instead of watching the video of themselves running away from the angry naked people on the beach, they'd see the ferret.

In his litter box.

Making a big ferret turd.

I tried to imagine the expressions on their faces.

Before we could sneak back into the house through the window, we had to wait until we stopped laughing. Even Richard.

chapterseventeen:

in which lillian is the life of yet another party or two messages

• • • • • • • • • • • •

The video images from the beach were downloadable by the next afternoon. One thing I'll say for Richard—he really knew what he was doing. I made sure he blurred out the naked people. They didn't deserve that kind of exposure. This was my final note on the Web site:

> To all my devoted fans,
>
> I trust you enjoyed your little glimpse into my world. My only hope is that through sharing this time with you, I was able to bring even a little color and light into your own dull, dreary, empty lives. Thanks for your interest, but as the saying goes, all good things must come to an end. You can go back to your video games now.
>
> In a way, I'll miss you.
>
> But not really.
>
> Sincerely,
> The Fabulous Floey Packer

Richard seemed to like that. He even laughed, which said a lot, considering he knew he couldn't go outside anymore. I almost felt sorry for him.

Almost.

In the last week of my cousins' visit, my mother was still mad about my hair. For two days she wouldn't even speak to me; we communicated through Post-it notes. But eventually she got over it. Tish was at my heels almost all the time. She wanted to do whatever I did, which was too bad for her because I didn't have any friends anymore, so I didn't have much of a life. We played cards and went for bike rides and watched movies. Sometimes, when we were feeling charitable, we even let Richard join us.

I was dreading Friday. The plan was, Aunt Sarah would fly in from Alaska and spend the night at our house and then she, Richard and Tish would catch a flight home Saturday evening. But, I consoled myself, once they were gone it would mean no more making breakfasts, cleaning bedrooms or babysitting. Soon my life could go back to normal.

Only, I was no longer sure what that meant. After all, I couldn't talk to Azra or Wen ever again. I dreaded going back to school at the end of the summer. I'd have to make a whole new set of friends. I'd also have to wonder, I supposed, which ones had seen the Web site.

Bright and wild like fire. Ha.

Friendless and alone like a pathetic loser was more like it.

A man asked a Zen master, "How does an enlightened one return to the ordinary world?" He answered, "A broken mirror never reflects again. Fallen flowers never go back to the branches."

If that was anybody, it was me.

• • •

When Aunt Sarah showed up at the terminal at Logan, I hardly recognized her. She wore hiking boots and a backpack and had a raccoon tan from wearing sunglasses on mountaintops. Other than the area around her eyes, she was completely orange. The outdoorsy look didn't suit her sourpuss face.

"Hello, my darlings," she said, squeezing first Richard and then Tish. "I'm *so* glad you met me here. You don't know how much I've missed you both." She put her hand on my mother's cheek. "Grace, it's so lovely to see you. How can I thank you? You have no idea what this trip meant for me. I have a completely new outlook on life."

To me she just said, "Is that you, Floey?" She stared at my hair.

Then she handed me her giant backpack to carry for her.

At home, Ma made me lug the enormous backpack up to the house and into her room. Aunt Sarah would be sleeping with my mother. I dumped her stuff on the bed and nearly crashed into her as I left the room. She smiled, but it was a fake smile. An I-don't-like-you-and-we-both-know-it smile.

What was wrong with the woman?

I stepped around her and marched toward my room, where I intended to hide until the following night. But then I changed my mind. There was no point in living like this. Maybe she was going to be unreasonable, but I didn't want any part of it. I turned around.

Floey Packer didn't hide anymore.

Aunt Sarah was about to unzip her pack when I marched back in. She straightened when she saw me.

We stood face to face.

"Aunt Sarah," I said. "I'm sorry that the birthday thank-you note Azra sent you hurt your feelings. Even though I didn't write it, I still should have called you or sent another note to clear it up. I'm sorry I didn't. But I still don't think you have any right to jump to conclusions about me, and you definitely shouldn't treat me like I'm some kind of delinquent when you don't even know me. *That's* rude and ignorant."

She narrowed her eyes, her hands on her hips. "Are you finished?"

I tried to think of something else to say but I couldn't. "Yes," I said, a little less sure of myself all of a sudden.

I thought she was going to lash out at me, maybe threaten to say something to my mother. But that's when Ma called me from the kitchen. "Floey! Come help me, please!"

Aunt Sarah kept glaring at me. "You better go, then," she said.

So I left.

For the rest of the day, she and I pretended the whole thing had never happened.

• • •

Lillian and Helmut came home later that night, exhausted and happy. Lillian screamed with laughter when she saw my new hair. "What happened to you, Floey? You look like a big purple cabbage!"

Personally, I'd had enough with the vegetable comments.

The sleeping arrangements were kind of ridiculous because we didn't have room for everyone. But my sister insisted on sleeping at home.

"I'm really moving away now, don't you get it? I'm moving to New York on Monday and I'll never ever live here ever again. Of *course* I don't want to stay in a *hotel*! Are you *kidding*?"

So Lillian and her new husband spent the first night after their honeymoon on our living room sofa. With the pillows off the back it's kind of a deep sofa, but still I don't think it could have been comfortable for the two of them.

Since Aunt Sarah and my cousins were flying home Saturday night, my mother prepared a truckload of food. Saturday would be the only remaining time we would all be together, so she wanted to have a picnic.

Saturday morning, I got up later than everyone else. Aunt Sarah was already packing Richard's stuff, Helmut was relaxing in the yard and Lillian was glued to the bathroom mirror, getting ready to present herself. As far as I knew, she hadn't actually phoned any of her friends to remind them she was back, but I knew, and she did too, that they'd be dropping by to see her today. While she brushed her hair and adjusted her makeup (she takes a *looong* time), I stood in the bathroom doorway and told her about my adventures: about Wen and Kim, Calvin, the Devil's Coffeehouse, the Old Naked People, Dean Eagler, the Web site, even Wen and Azra. I didn't tell her about Richard's bed-wetting problem, though. I had a promise to keep.

"Wow, Floey," she said. "I'm impressed. I guess my baby sister is having herself quite a summer."

"I guess so," I said, happy that she thought so.

"Wen, Calvin *and* Dean Eagler?" She shook her head at me, pretending to be shocked. "This won't do. You'll have to tone it down or you'll catch up to me. We can't have that, now, can we?"

Actually, I wasn't worried. I knew I'd never catch up to her.

Just for a laugh, she leaned over and gave me a bright apricot lipstick kiss on my forehead. "More power to you, kid. Dealing with multiple guys is like juggling. No matter what happens, keep them all up in the air." Then she made fish lips at me. She thought she was so funny.

"Do you really think," I asked her, wiping my face with a tissue, "that you and Helmut will be in love forever?"

She wrinkled her nose. "Of course. What a question."

"It's not so weird. If you look around at the people we know, doesn't it kind of seem like it's hard to stay happy for a whole lifetime?"

"Listen, little girl," she said, frowning. "You don't know anything about anything." She took out her lipstick again, leaned into the mirror and pursed her lips.

I stared at her, amazed. I had to laugh.

"What's funny?"

"Nothing," I said. "It's just that I like your answer. It's very Zen."

She frowned again.

• • •

Frank Sinatra nibbled on my toes while I sat on the front steps. He was acting friendly, but only because he wanted my breakfast. Every now and then I tossed him some of my cereal. The humidity had passed, the sky was bright and cheerful and I only had a few more hours until Aunt Sarah would be gone gone gone.

Things were looking up. Everything was coming up roses.

Except not really.

I hadn't been able to bring myself even to think about Wen all week, let alone phone him. And in the past few days somebody had called at least seven times and then when I said "Hello" they hung up. I knew it was Azra. On one of the last calls I could hear her mother in the background. I wondered what she wanted. Why didn't she talk? I even called her once. I'd decided to tell her that I missed her and that we should stay best friends. I got her machine, though. And while I listened to her mother's voice I found myself thinking about Azra and Wen and how they were probably together right then. Before the machine got to the beep, I hung up.

I didn't really want to talk to her anyway.

I wondered miserably if we would ever be friends again. Or if I still wanted us to be.

And that's what I was thinking about when the door opened and I felt a cold, gloomy presence hovering behind me. Aunt Sarah. I didn't say a word, and neither did she. I went back to eating my cereal. Eventually, she sat down beside me.

Frank Sinatra ran as far as his harness would take him. Smart ferret.

"So, what are you eating, kiddo?" she asked. She was obviously trying to start a casual conversation with me, but she sounded uncomfortable. No surprise. What a stupid way to begin. And why pretend we were friends? Why couldn't she just leave me alone? The woman was a loon.

I tipped my bowl in her direction so she could see. Then I kept eating.

"Listen, Floey. I was talking with your mother. She said you worked hard taking care of Richard and Tish. I want to thank you for that."

"Mmmm."

There's a Zen saying: When left with nothing to say, rest content in the knowledge that there is really nothing to say.

"No, I mean it. I really appreciate it. And I hope they didn't give you and your mother too much trouble while I was gone."

Oh, if she only knew.

After another uncomfortable silence, she blew out a long breath and shifted her weight. I still kept quiet. If she was here to apologize, which she absolutely ought to be, why should I make it easy for her?

"So anyway," she continued, "I just want to tell you that I don't think you're a delinquent. I'm sorry if I made you feel that way."

Blah blah blah.

I shrugged. "It doesn't matter to me what you think. You

can think whatever you want. Okay, so I'm not a delinquent, I'm just some terrible, ungrateful person. I don't care."

"Floey, I don't think you're a terrible person."

Yeah yeah.

"Whatever. You have no idea what I'm really like. How could you when you haven't seen me in years? You don't know me at all."

She stared at me. "I know," she said finally. "I know."

I went back to my cereal.

"So you think I haven't been a very good aunt, is that it? Maybe I should have visited more often?"

I shrugged. What was I supposed to say to that?

"Floey, you don't know me, either. We all have our own problems. Your mother knows that airplanes fly in both directions, you know."

All right. That was true.

And then she totally and utterly surprised me.

"Well, in case you're interested, I have an idea. The summer isn't over yet, so why don't you come and stay with us for a week or so sometime before school starts? I'll pay for your flight and I'll show you around Chicago. It'd give us a chance to get to know each other."

I nearly fell off the stairs.

What was she thinking? Why would I want to do that?

"You don't have to answer now. Think about it."

"Thanks," I said, amazed. "Only I don't think I can do it. I . . . I have a lot going on."

"Fine," she said. "If it doesn't work out this summer, you have an open invitation. Just let me know."

I gaped at her. Could the woman making this suggestion really be my aunt Sarah, the woman who hated me? I had visions of arriving in Chicago and immediately being locked in her basement and tortured.

She took off her floppy hat and fiddled with the edges. "I guess a training bra is kind of a dumb gift, isn't it?"

I studied her face. Was she telling me that she knew it, or was she asking me? Finally, I said, "Yes, it kind of is."

One side of her mouth smiled.

"But you were just trying to be nice," I said.

"That's true. I *was*." She fanned herself now with the hat. "I thought I knew something about thirteen-year-old girls, but I guess I only remembered how it was for *me*. At thirteen I certainly didn't need a real bra, like you. After all," she said, "I barely need one now."

And then she laughed.

And I smiled, but just a little.

• • •

Helmut set up chairs and blankets in the field behind our house and we all helped bring out the food. Even before we'd finished setting everything up, Lillian's friends started to arrive. Rebecca Greenblatt came first, followed by other friends and admirers. God only knew where Lillian had met them all. Some of them I recognized, some I didn't, but Lillian greeted them all like they were her best friends. Frida and Digger waved to me. Almost everybody brought food. Thankfully, Billy Fishman never showed his face.

It was a beautiful summer day. For a while, Mrs. Horowitz and I talked about the wedding. Nearby, Helmut was too busy eating to say much to anybody. I wondered if he forgot to eat in Mexico. Admirers crowded around my sister. She looked comfortable and happy and in her element. She was the queen bee, a completely different animal than me.

I was deep in thought, watching her, when somebody put a hand on my shoulder. "Hiya, Floey. What's the news?"

"Oh, hello, Gary," I said.

Something over my shoulder caught his eye, so I turned to see. At the other side of the crowd, my mother was talking to somebody in front of the table with the paper plates and plastic cups and utensils. She noticed us and waved. Gary waved back.

I thought of the Old Naked People. Maybe Lillian was right and I didn't know anything. One thing I was sure of, though, was that I wanted my mother to have somebody to go skinny-dipping with in her old age.

"Keep working on her," I said to him, taking his hand and walking him over to her. "I'll start working on her too."

He turned bright red.

Everybody pretty much stopped talking as soon as Lillian began telling stories about her trip. By then, I'd drifted to the back of the crowd, unnoticed again. But this time it was okay—I wanted to sneak away for a while. In the house, I grabbed the two things I'd prepared before the party and put them into a plastic bag. I was going for a bike ride.

I had some things to do, things I needed to set right.

First, I pedaled toward the secret beach. Once I turned down the path, I got off my bike and crept up to the little cottage. I carefully slipped a letter into the mailbox.

To the People Who Used This House for Most of July (Please Forward as Appropriate):

I'm sorry I disturbed you while you were swimming the other night. Actually, there was one other time, maybe you remember it, and I'm sorry about that too. I won't do it again. I promise.

I hope your true love lasts and lasts.

Sincerely,
Anonymous

I got back on my bike and continued.

With no camp on Saturdays, I figured I might find Azra at home. By the time I reached her house I was feeling pretty anxious. At the end of her driveway I stopped, still straddling my bike.

Leaning against her garage door was Wen's bicycle.

If he was in there too, I wasn't so sure I wanted to see them. Maybe someday I'd be okay with them being a couple, but not yet. Still, I'd already come all the way over here with Smiley Quahog. I decided to leave him on the front step and then ride away. She'd find him and get the message, but I wouldn't have to see them together. Not just yet.

I set my bike down on the lawn and crept up to the front door. I put the little swordsman directly in front of the welcome mat so she wouldn't miss him. Then I turned and started running back to my bike.

Before I got halfway down the driveway, I heard the screen door squeak.

"Thanks," Azra's voice called out.

I turned around. She'd seen me, so there was no point in trying to get away now.

She picked up the quahog and held it in her hand. "Does this mean you're not mad at me anymore?"

I didn't say anything right away. I shrugged. "I don't know. Does that mean you're not mad at *me* anymore?"

She just stood there.

I felt like running away again.

But then Wen stepped into view behind her. He looked a little uncomfortable, but at the same time he seemed happy to see me. "Why don't you come inside?" he said after a moment. "We're just goofing around."

"Can't." I took a couple of backward steps toward my bike. Leslie Dern appeared in the doorway then, looking different from how I'd ever seen her. In the emotion of the moment, I didn't notice why. "I have to go," I said.

Nobody said anything else for a few seconds. It was really strange.

Finally, I said, "Bye." And then I left.

A block away, I started to hate myself for leaving. But on the other hand, I was the one who'd biked all the way out there. Azra should have made more of an effort.

Halfway home I heard another bike racing behind me. It was Wen.

I stopped for him. "Floey!" he called. "I'd really hate it if we ended up not being friends anymore!"

I didn't want to admit it, but I was incredibly happy that he'd followed me. I looked behind him to see if anybody else was coming over the hill. Maybe Azra?

As soon as he was close enough for us to talk, he stopped. He was a little out of breath. As if he'd read my mind, he shook his head. "Just me."

I tried not to look disappointed.

"Look," he said. "I just wanted to tell you I'm sorry for causing so much trouble. I never meant to hurt you. Azra didn't either. Right now I think she's only acting hurt and angry because she doesn't know what else to do. I think she's really more sad than anything else. She wants to fix this, but she doesn't know how. Me neither."

I didn't know what to say.

He leaned forward on his handlebars. "I . . . I hope you don't hate us forever."

"I don't hate you," I said. "Look, it's okay. I'll get over it."

"I just want us to be friends, like before."

I shook my head. "I don't think that's really possible, do you? Everything is kind of different now."

He looked so sad. "Different, okay. Maybe not like before. But still friends?"

I shrugged again. "I guess I'd like that. I don't know if Azra would, though."

"Floey, why don't you come back with me to the house?"

"No, I really can't. Lillian's home and my cousins are leaving. We're having a goodbye party and I have to get back to it." After a few more seconds of staring at each other I couldn't stand it anymore. "I really have to go," I said. I hopped back onto the seat of my bike. "Listen, there's a lot of food. You guys should come on over, if you want. Leslie too."

He didn't say anything at first, but then he said, "I'll have to work on Azra. Maybe."

"Either way," I said, pedaling off. "It doesn't matter."

As soon as I was out of sight I had to stop. My hands were shaking.

• • •

I'd been gone less than an hour but for once my mother noticed. As soon as I got back she found me. "There you are! I was just looking for you. One minute you were here and the next you were gone. Come back with me. Wait by that tree. I asked Gary to take some pictures."

It took her forever to gather my extended family, especially Lillian. My sister loves to have her picture taken but hates to wait. She kept wandering away and gabbing. Eventually, Gary managed to position us around one of the big trees at the side of our field. He put Richard and Tish on one of the two big low branches and Lillian, Helmut and me on the other. In front of the trunk he put my mom and Aunt Sarah.

I got it. A family tree.

Richard had brought Frank Sinatra over to Lillian so she

could put him in her lap, but when she tried to take him he hissed at her and ran away. By then there was a big crowd in our yard, bigger than at the wedding. Lillian should run for president someday. She'd win. I scanned the heads for Azra or Wen but didn't see them yet. I craned my neck to see the road, hoping I might catch them when they arrived. If they arrived.

Which they probably wouldn't.

"Hey!" Lillian shrieked. "Floey's not even looking at the camera! Floey!"

Suddenly and unexpectedly, I felt a wave of emotion for my sister. She was really leaving home for good. I'd had almost four weeks without her, but it hadn't really seemed final until now. But now I missed her even though she was right next to me. I wasn't the only emotional one either. Gary's eyes were tearing up again.

I forced myself to smile so he could snap the picture.

Just then, though, Richard tried to push Tish off the branch, but she kept her balance. She pushed him right back. When he hit the ground, Aunt Sarah and my mother gasped and started yelling at Tish. But Richard wasn't hurt. I couldn't help laughing. Tish laughed so hard she snorted.

That's when I had another sudden strange realization: when Tish left, I was going to feel sad. I kind of liked the way she followed me around and kept me awake with her stupid, nosy questions. It was kind of like having a little sister.

Back on his branch, Richard the boy genius crossed his eyes and flared his nostrils at me. Would I miss him, too?

Probably not.

• • •

Later, I was talking with one of Lillian's friends when somebody tapped my shoulder.

"How many Zen masters does it take to screw in a lightbulb?"

I turned around. Azra looked nervous, but she was holding out Smiley Quahog for me. "None," I said, grinning. "They're already enlightened."

Over her shoulder, at the end of the yard, I saw Wen watching us. I wondered if this meant everything was going back to normal again.

But then I spotted Leslie next to Wen. Finally, I noticed what was different. How could I have missed it before? Her hair had new streaks of color. Violet.

Then I remembered.

Normal didn't mean much anymore.

chapter eighteen:

impermanence

• • • • • • • • • • • •

There had already been seven separate toddlers tearing around the waiting room. They'd climbed behind the desk, pulled open the stationery boxes and screamed at their parents and each other. Gary had asked me to cover the reception area. Sunday morning is always a busy time for family portraits, especially families with small children.

It was my job to be pleasant.

Now, two little kids waiting with their tired-looking father were throwing their shoes at each other and shrieking. I was standing behind the desk, using it as a shield.

Another hour to go and my nerves were already shattered.

That's when I noticed Calvin standing outside. He was peering through the window, his cowboy hat touching the glass. When he saw me notice him, he grinned.

I'd been thinking about him a lot, wondering if he was ever going to write to me again, maybe even send me more of his poems. I'd searched the mail every day, hoping to find an envelope with his name on it. Now here he was, walking through the door and up to the desk.

I wished I were wearing something nicer.

"Floey, is that you?" he said slowly, staring at my head. "Wow."

"I know, I know," I said, ready for the comments. "I look like a giant grape Popsicle, right?" I'd been considering dying it brown again, but that morning I'd decided to keep it violet for now. Not because it made me stand out—I didn't care about that as much anymore. I just liked it.

He smiled. "No. I think it looks great, I really do."

I tried to decide if he was making fun of me. He didn't sound like it. He seemed sincere. Eventually, he stopped staring at my head and looked me in the eyes. "But I liked you without it too."

I stared back. "Thanks."

Right then a little blue shoe hit him in the back of the head. *Thump.*

The children shrieked with laughter.

Calvin looked surprised, but he calmly turned around, picked up the shoe and handed it to the embarrassed father, who apologized and then spoke sternly to the children. Calvin turned back to me and rubbed his head.

"Written anything lately?"

"As a matter of fact, yes. I started something new yesterday. But it's not a poem, it's a story."

"Really? What's it about?"

"My summer. It's been kind of a weird one."

He gave me a half smile. "Mine too."

The boy, who was obviously ignoring his father, climbed up onto one of the chairs and, in a pirate voice, announced to his sister that she was going to have to walk the plank. The girl screamed and tried to run between Calvin's legs.

"I was here before," Calvin said over the noise. He stepped aside for the little girl. "Two other times. You weren't working."

He'd been back here twice? To see me?

"Avast ye, mateys!" the little boy said. "It's the dirty Spaniards! To the cannons!" I ducked. Another shoe whizzed by Calvin's ear. The children laughed. I guess they'd decided we were the Spanish Armada.

"Yikes!" Calvin said. He held up his hand to protect his head.

The father grabbed the children, one under each arm, and put them in the corner. I handed the shoe back to the poor man. "I'm so sorry," he said. "Really."

I smiled my biggest, sweetest smile. "It's no problem. Gary shouldn't be long. Would you like some water?"

"Kind of a dangerous job," Calvin said when I came back.

I leaned on the counter and grinned. "All in a day's work." After another silence I said, "So, why are you here?"

"I want to talk to you."

"You do? What about?"

There was yet another awkward silence. He put his hands in his pockets and kind of swayed anxiously back and forth before he finally spoke again.

"I . . . uh, Melanie and I broke up."

"You did? Why?"

And even more curiously, why was he telling *me*?

He glanced at the desk, the wall behind me, anywhere but at me. Then all of a sudden he took his hands out of his pockets, leaned across the counter and kissed me. I was so surprised. My first real kiss was soft and sweet. The whole thing only lasted a few seconds, but in my mind I've relived it at least a thousand times. An instant later I found myself staring at him, wide-eyed. He looked nervously back at me.

"Calvin, why did you do that?"

"I've been thinking of doing it for a long time."

"But what about what you said? I'm only thirteen, remember? And you're going to be a sophomore."

He shrugged. "I know. But you'll be a freshman when I'm a junior, right?"

I nodded.

That's when the door opened and a young couple with twin babies dressed in frilly pink outfits entered and stood waiting for me. At the same time, the family Gary had been photographing charged back into the waiting area.

"Look," Calvin said over the sudden increase in noise, "I know you have to work. Thing is, I keep thinking about you, Floey. I'd really like to see you sometime."

I was so shocked that for a moment I couldn't speak.

Still standing in the corner, his head leaning against the wall, the little boy started singing a song:

"Give me a snot sandwich on a dirty dish,
French fried worms and a side of dead fish."

I pulled myself together. "A week from tomorrow there's another poetry night. I was thinking about going."

"Good. Great. See you there, then."

The little girl laughed and joined in the song with her brother.

"Frogs that squish and bugs that crunch—
That's what I want for lunch!"

A moment later, the door opened and closed, and with a wave through the window, Calvin was gone. I barely heard the new family give me their names. I could have risen right off the floor and floated away.

But then I had a sudden terrible thought.

I wanted to ignore it, but after only a few seconds I just couldn't.

With the family still standing right in front of me, I stepped out from behind the desk and ran to the door. By that time, Calvin was a few cars into the parking lot.

"Calvin!" I called. He turned around. "What made you send me that note—the one with the haiku? Did you write it because of the Web site?"

"Web site? What do you mean?"

"You don't know anything about it?"

He shrugged and shook his head. "I don't know what you're talking about."

I wasn't sure if I should believe him. I tried to see if there was anything in his face or his posture that might give him away.

But then I got ahold of myself.

I was thinking too much again. Hadn't he just told me he didn't know about the Web site? He *seemed* sincere, didn't he? And hadn't he come to the studio *three times* just to see *me*? And even if he had read my diary, he was gorgeous gorgeous gorgeous. So who *cared*?

This Zen cowboy was *my* Zen cowboy.

If he was interested in me, who was I to object?

And most importantly, I believed him.

Now, *that's* enlightenment.

• • •

On Monday afternoon I didn't know what to do with myself. In the end I went out to the backyard, lay down in the grass and stared up at the sky. I had a lot to think about.

So many changes all at once.

At the airport only two days before, I'd waved to Tish as she walked with Richard and Aunt Sarah through the gate. I'm terrible at goodbyes. It'd been harder than I thought it would be.

And then there was this morning.

After Helmut had staggered down the stairs with my sister's gigantic suitcases, Lillian had hugged my mother and me, tears streaming down her face. I knew she wasn't really sad, though. She and Helmut looked happy. We'd visit them soon enough, I knew. And then they'd pulled out of our driveway and headed toward New York and the rest of their lives.

As I stared up at the sky, I missed my sister so much it almost hurt. But I was glad for her. Really, I was.

I was glad for me, too. It seemed like Azra and Wen and I were friends again. Not only that, but I was pretty sure I had a boyfriend. Only this time I wasn't going to tell anyone about it until I was absolutely positive.

In his outside harness, Frank Sinatra nuzzled around happily on my stomach. At least *he* wasn't leaving my life just yet. After he'd nipped Helmut's hand, Ma had suggested that Lillian leave him with me—at least until she and Helmut got settled into their new apartment. Lillian had reluctantly agreed.

I'd brought my diary, and now I took it out.

Monday, July 28, 3:15 p.m.

To the Extraordinary Floey Packer,

I still believe in you. Wallpaper or not, whoever you turn out to be, I know you'll be special and remarkable. Even though I don't have everything figured out yet, I know if I stick around long enough you'll eventually show up. Not that I'm just going to sit around until you do. While I'm waiting, I have a few new things I want to try.

For starters, I'm going to see what Chicago's like. After that, maybe I'll write a book.

Yours expectantly,
Floey

For a while the ferret and I both stared up at the blue sky and white clouds. Suddenly, my mother's face blocked the view.

"There you are," she said. "I've been looking for you."

"I've been right here."

After a moment, she sat down next to me in the grass. "So it's just you and me now. How does it feel?"

"Weird," I said.

She nodded and looked away. Her fingers pulled softly at the grass. Finally, she smiled and said, "I'm sure we'll both get used to it."

Then I remembered that Gary had offered to take us to the movies. I'd told him I didn't want to go, but I figured Ma would.

"Are you and Gary going out tonight?"

She shook her head. "I took a rain check. Tonight I have a special quiet evening planned, just for us. What do you say we sit and talk over sushi?"

"Sounds great," I said, surprised. "I'd like that." But she wasn't done. I could tell from her face that there was more. "And then?"

She grinned and held up a DVD. *Viva Las Vegas*, another Elvis favorite.

I smiled.

I guess some things never change.

About the Author

Mark Peter Hughes was born in Liverpool, England, but grew up in the coastal town of Barrington, Rhode Island. He attributes his ability to write from a female perspective to growing up in a house dominated by "an extroverted mother and two wildly verbal sisters who rarely showed any shyness about expressing whatever was on their minds."

As a teenager, Mark worked in many different jobs: gas station attendant, fast-food zombie, beach sticker enforcer, dishwasher ("I was fired after only two days"), clam factory worker ("this was the smelliest of jobs—my sisters avoided me all summer"), and movie theater usher, among others. A former member of a local alternative rock band, he was once kicked out of eighth-grade music class for throwing a spitball.

He left Rhode Island to attend the University of Rochester, where he earned a degree in engineering with a minor in creative writing. Mark now lives in Wayland, Massachusetts, with his wife, Karen, and their three small children: Evan, Lucía, and Zoe. He has written stories ever since he can remember.

Check out Mark's Web site at www.markpeterhughes.com.

★ "Floey Packer, thirteen, bursts right off the page with an engaging vivacity. First-time author Hughes merits a place with Louise Rennison, Ellen Conford, and even Paula Danziger on the fiction shelves."
—*School Library Journal*, Starred

markpeterhughes

A Readers Guide

Questions for Discussion

1. On page 40, Floey declares to her diary, "The days of the invisible, ordinary, wallpaper Floey Packer are over. Tonight marks the birth of a whole new me." Why does Floey decide to change herself? Compare the way she feels at the beginning of her sister Lillian's wedding day with the way she feels at the end. Have you ever felt as if there's something about you that you'd like to change?

2. Describe Floey's relationships with her mother and her sister. As Lillian is getting married, what different emotions do you think her mother might have? How about Lillian herself? How do their actions suggest these emotions to you?

3. Friendships play an important role in the book. Compare Floey's friendships with Azra, Wen, and Calvin. What do you think each friend provides that makes him or her unique?

4. What role does Zen Buddhism play in Floey's transformation? Do you think Floey truly comprehends the concepts introduced? How does her behavior demonstrate her understanding, or lack of understanding, of Zen?

5. When Floey discovers floeysprivatelife.com, how does she, as the "new" Floey, react? How do you think the "old" Floey might have responded? Have you ever kept a diary? What would you do if it was exposed to the public?

6. Discuss what Richard sets in motion with his part in creating floeysprivatelife.com. Is he justified in getting back at Floey this way? Can you imagine different results of the site's creation and popularity? Do you think Richard understands what he is doing to Floey by exposing her in this way?

7. On page 42, in the chapter title, Floey describes her cousins as "children from hell." Do you think this characterization is justified? How would you describe Floey's initial behavior toward her cousins? Do you think her treatment of them affects what happens to her later?

8. On pages 219 and 220, Floey reflects on the way she feels about her cousins leaving. She decides she'll miss Tish, and she wonders about Richard, "Would I miss him, too? Probably not." How accurate do you think Floey's prediction is? Is she being overly harsh about Richard, or just honest?

9. How has Floey changed by the end of the book? Has she become the kind of person she intended to turn into when she first envisioned the "new" Floey? Do you think her goals for herself have changed?

10. Floey concludes the book with the observation "I guess some things never change" (page 228). What do you think will change for Floey in the coming school year? What will happen to her friendships with Wen, Azra, and Calvin?

A Conversation with Mark Peter Hughes

Q: *I Am the Wallpaper* is written from the perspective of Floey Packer, a thirteen-year-old girl. Never having been a thirteen-year-old girl, how did you conceive of Floey's voice? What made you want to write from the point of view of the opposite sex?

A: I didn't actually set out with the goal of writing from the point of view of a girl. The novel grew out of a short story I wrote in college in which a teenager feels humiliated by having to sit at the children's table during her sister's wedding reception. But it was Floey's tenacious character that appealed to me and made me want to pursue her story, not the fact that she was a girl. As I was writing, it didn't occur to me that it might be seen as an unusual perspective for me to write from. I was just working on a story about a character I found interesting. If I got any of the girl-specific details right, it may have been partly because I grew up with two sisters.

As for how I found Floey's voice, I spent a lot of time writing out her diary. I probably wrote hundreds of pages, very little of which actually ended up in the book. But it was an important step because that was how I eventually discovered who she was.

Q: Did you ever keep a diary?

A: Yes, but only in intermittent periods throughout my childhood. One problem was that I worried that one of my sisters might discover it and read whatever I'd written. In fact, that scenario never actually happened, but it was a concern. Also, I never had the discipline to keep up the routine of writing down my thoughts on a daily basis.

Q: Tell us about Floey's writing. Why haiku?

A: Haiku are wonderful because they can squeeze so much into so little. They're tiny nuggets capable of expressing giant thoughts or deep emotions. But with only a few syllables to work with, every word has to count. I guess that's why I felt that Floey, who starts the novel with a lot to say but feeling like she doesn't keep anybody's attention for long, would naturally gravitate to haiku as a way of documenting the various steps in her personal journey as she tries to reach for something higher. Plus, they're a lot of fun to write.

Q: And the idea of a private diary made public over the Internet?

A: That came from thinking about how we all value our privacy even though we live in a hyperconnected new world where it can be so very easy (*too* easy, perhaps) to share information with strangers through technology. I think a lot of people are only just beginning to realize some of the implications—how powerful an effect this new technology can have on our lives, both good and bad.

Q: There's been a lot of talk in the press recently about cyberbullying, kids using instant messages, e-mail, and the Internet to bully classmates. Do you think Floey's experience qualifies as cyberbullying? Why do you think she decides to handle it as she does, without telling any parents or authorities?

A: Absolutely this qualifies as cyberbullying. What Billy and Richard do is truly creepy. I wanted that creepiness to be reflected in the story. I wanted to suggest how vulnerable our own personal information can be in cyberspace, while not taking the story into the darker direction it could have gone under different circumstances. I think Floey recognizes the seriousness of the situation, though, and understands the kind of trouble the boys could get into. When she chooses to address the situation on her own, I think she makes that decision partly out of a sense of guilt for the way she treated her cousins when they arrived, partly because of the developing connection she already feels with Tish, and partly because, as terribly as the boys have behaved, on some level Floey recognizes that they're just little kids. In Floey's case, this go-it-alone approach ends up working out. But certainly if anybody experiences real-life cyberbullying I would urge them to consider seeking outside help.

Q: Zen Buddhism plays a big role in Floey's conversion into the "new" Floey. How do you think it helps her cope with all the terrible things she learns over the course of the summer? What made you want to include Zen Buddhism as the guiding light in Floey's transformation?

A: I'm fascinated by Zen Buddhism but I'm not an expert on it and neither is Floey. And perhaps that's the point. Reaching out and trying something unfamiliar is a surefire pathway to personal growth. Floey makes an active decision to step out of herself and become something new. The constructs of Zen—the ideas of connectedness and karma and impermanence and meditation—present her with an intriguing new framework for approaching complicated questions and thinking about life in general. To me it's not important whether she pursues it further in her life. What's important is that for right now, for this summer, it helps her frame her situation and envision the possibilities.

Q: What are you working on now? Will Floey turn up in another novel, or will you revisit the town of Opequonsett?

A: Yes, Opequonsett, Rhode Island, is also the setting for my next novel, *Lemonade Mouth*. And yes, Floey does make a brief appearance. *Lemonade Mouth* is about five high school outcasts who meet in detention, decide to form the weirdest band ever, and then try to change the world. It's told from five different perspectives, one of which is the perspective of Wen from *I Am the Wallpaper*. Music has always played an important part in my life, as has the state of Rhode Island. I especially love the weird little details about the place. For example, did you know that Rhode Island is the home of the Ukulele Hall of Fame? How cool is *that*?

Girl, 15, Charming but Insane
Sue Limb
978-0-385-73215-4
With her hilariously active imagination, Jess Jordan has a tendency to complicate her life, but now, as she's finally getting closer to her crush, she's determined to keep things under control. Readers will fall in love with Sue Limb's insanely optimistic heroine.

The Unlikely Romance of Kate Bjorkman
Louise Plummer
978-0-375-89521-0
I'm Kate Bjorkman. I don't like romance novels. They're full of three-paragraph kisses describing people's tongues and spittle. But I wrote this romance novel about myself, using *The Romance Writer's Phrase Book.* This is the honest truth, and I want truth even in romance. I'm betting you'll want the same.

related titles

The Sisterhood of the Traveling Pants
Ann Brashares
978-0-385-73058-7
Over a few bags of cheese puffs, four girls decide to form a sisterhood and take the vow of the Sisterhood of the Traveling Pants. The next morning, they say goodbye. And then the journey of the Pants, and the most memorable summer of their lives, begin.

Stargirl
Jerry Spinelli
978-0-375-82233-9
Stargirl. From the day she arrives at quiet Mica High in a burst of color and sound, the hallways hum with the murmur of "Stargirl, Stargirl." The students are enchanted. Then they turn on her.

A Great and Terrible Beauty
Libba Bray
978-0-385-73231-4
Sixteen-year-old Gemma Doyle is sent to the Spence Academy in London after tragedy strikes her family in India. Lonely, guilt-ridden, and prone to visions of the future that have an uncomfortable habit of coming true, Gemma finds her reception a chilly one. But at Spence, Gemma's power to attract the supernatural unfolds; she becomes entangled with the school's most powerful girls and discovers her mother's connection to a shadowy group called the Order. A curl-up-under-the-covers Victorian gothic.

Counting Stars
David Almond
978-0-440-41826-9
With stories that shimmer and vibrate in the bright heat of memory, David Almond creates a glowing mosaic of his life growing up in a large, loving Catholic family in northeastern England.

Before We Were Free
Julia Alvarez
978-0-440-23784-6
Under a dictatorship in the Dominican Republic in 1960, young Anita lives through a fight for freedom that changes her world forever.

The Chocolate War
Robert Cormier
978-0-375-82987-1
Jerry Renault dares to disturb the universe in this groundbreaking and now classic novel, an unflinching portrait of corruption and cruelty in a boys' prep school.

Dr. Franklin's Island
Ann Halam
978-0-440-23781-5
A plane crash leaves Semi, Miranda, and Arnie stranded on a tropical island, totally alone. Or so they think. Dr. Franklin is a mad scientist who has set up his laboratory on the island, and the three teens are perfect subjects for his frightening experiments in genetic engineering.

Keeper of the Night
Kimberly Willis Holt
978-0-553-49441-9
Living on the island of Guam, a place lush with memories and tradition, young Isabel struggles to protect her family and cope with growing up after her mother's suicide.

When Zachary Beaver Came to Town
Kimberly Willis Holt
978-0-440-23841-6
Toby's small, sleepy Texas town is about to get a jolt with the arrival of Zachary Beaver, billed as the fattest boy in the world. Toby is in for a summer unlike any other—a summer sure to change his life.

The Parallel Universe of Liars
Kathleen Jeffrie Johnson
978-0-440-23852-2
Surrounded by superficiality, infidelity, and lies, Robin, a self-described chunk, isn't sure what to make of her hunky neighbor's sexual advances, or of the attention paid her by a new boy in town who seems to notice more than her body.

Ghost Boy
Iain Lawrence
978-0-440-41668-5
Fourteen-year-old Harold Kline is an albino—an outcast. When the circus comes to town, Harold runs off to join it in hopes of discovering who he is and what he wants in life. Is he a circus freak or just a normal guy?

The Lightkeeper's Daughter
Iain Lawrence
978-0-385-73127-0
Imagine growing up on a tiny island with no one but your family. For Squid McCrae, returning to the island after three years away unleashes a storm of bittersweet memories, revelations, and accusations surrounding her brother's death.

Gathering Blue
Lois Lowry
978-0-385-73256-7
Lamed and suddenly orphaned, Kira is mysteriously taken to live in the palatial Council Edifice, where she is expected to use her gifts as a weaver to do the bidding of the all-powerful Guardians.

The Giver
Lois Lowry
978-0-385-73255-0
Jonas's world is perfect. Everything is under control. There is no war or fear or pain. There are no choices, until Jonas is given an opportunity that will change his world forever.

Shades of Simon Gray
Joyce McDonald
978-0-440-22804-2
Simon is the ideal teenager—smart, reliable, hardworking, trustworthy. Or is he? After Simon's car crashes into a tree and he slips into a coma, another portrait of him begins to emerge.

Zipped
Laura and Tom McNeal
978-0-375-83098-3
In a suspenseful novel of betrayal, forgiveness, and first love, fifteen-year-old Mick Nichols opens an e-mail he was never meant to see—
and learns a terrible secret.

Harmony
Rita Murphy
978-0-440-22923-0
Power is coursing through Harmony—the power to affect the universe with her energy. This is a frightening gift for a girl who has always hated being different, and Harmony must decide whether to hide her abilities or embrace the consequences—good and bad—of her full strength.

Cuba 15
Nancy Osa
978-0-385-73233-8
Violet Paz's upcoming *quinceañero,* a girl's traditional fifteenth-birthday coming-of-age ceremony, awakens her interest in her Cuban roots—and sparks a fire of conflicting feelings about Cuba within her family.

Both Sides Now
Ruth Pennebaker
978-0-440-22933-9
A compelling look at breast cancer through the eyes of a mother and daughter. Liza must learn a few life lessons from her mother, Rebecca, about the power of family.

Her Father's Daughter
Mollie Poupeney
978-0-440-22879-0
As she matures from a feisty tomboy of seven to a spirited young woman of fourteen, Maggie discovers that the only constant in her life of endless new homes and new faces is her ever-emerging sense of herself.

Pool Boy
Michael Simmons
978-0-385-73196-6
Brett Gerson is the kind of guy you love to hate—until his father is thrown in prison and Brett has to give up the good life. That's when some swimming pools enter his world and change everything.

Milkweed
Jerry Spinelli
978-0-440-42005-7
He's a boy called Jew. Gypsy. Stopthief. Runt. He's a boy who lives in the streets of Warsaw. He's a boy who wants to be a Nazi someday, with tall, shiny jackboots of his own. Until the day that suddenly makes him change his mind—the day he realizes it's safest of all to be nobody.

Memories of Summer
Ruth White
978-0-440-22921-6
In 1955, thirteen-year-old Lyric describes her older sister Summer's descent into mental illness, telling Summer's story with humor, courage, and love.